Married to the man she met at eighteen, **Susanne Hampton** is the mother of two adult daughters—one a musician and the other an artist. Susanne loves everything romantic and pretty, so her home is brimming with romance novels, movies and shoes. With her interest in all things medical, her career has been in the dental field and the medical world in different roles—and now Susanne has taken that love into writing Mills & Boon Medical Romance.

### Books by Susanne Hampton

### Mills & Boon Medical Romance

*Unlocking the Doctor's Heart*
*Back in Her Husband's Arms*
*Falling for Dr December*
*Midwife's Baby Bump*
*A Baby to Bind Them*

Visit the Author Profile page
at millsandboon.co.uk for more titles.

As I was putting the final touches to this book I was given the news that my amazing editor Charlotte was moving along her career pathway and would no longer be working with me. So this will be my final dedication to her and my last written recognition of her guidance, patience, much needed honesty and unwavering belief in my work. However, what I have learnt from her over the last five books will travel with me on my writing journey, so in many ways all of my books and writing success in the future will be a dedication to Charlotte Mursell.

Thank you, Charlotte.

### Praise for Susanne Hampton

'From the first turbulent beginning until the final climactic ending, an entire range of emotions has been used to write a story of two people travelling the rocky road to love…an excellent story. I would recommend this story to all romance readers.'
—*Contemporary Romance Reviews* on
*Unlocking the Doctor's Heart*

'I recommend this read for all fans of medical romance. It's the perfect balance: spunky, emotional, heartfelt, a very sweet and tender romance with a great message!'
—*Contemporary Romance Reviews* on
*Unlocking the Doctor's Heart*

# CHAPTER ONE

DR HEATH ROLLINS momentarily looked away from the emails on his laptop computer, across the living room of the family home, to see his father sitting by the lace dressed bay window in his favourite armchair. With the mid-morning sunlight streaming into the room, he was intently reading the paper. Heath smiled a bittersweet smile as his gaze roamed to the old oversized chair, upholstered in green and blue tartan. It was a piece of furniture his mother had tried to have re-covered or removed from their home for many years but Ken Rollins had been adamant that it stayed. And stayed exactly as it was. It was a Clan Sutherland tartan, of the Highland Clans of Scotland, Heath would hear his father tell his mother, and it had direct links to the maternal side of his family. She would tell him that family connections or not, it was an extremely unattractive chair that looked out of place in their new French provincial decor. Frankly, it was hideous and it just didn't belong.

His mother and father had argued about very little except that chair. But, unlike all those years ago, now his father was stuck in that now slightly worn chair for hours on end, his leg elevated and his knee freshly dressed after surgery. And there were no more arguments about the chair as Heath's mother had passed away twenty years ago.

Heath then caught sight of his own suitcases, stacked against the hall wall, with the airline tags still intact. He would shortly be taking them to the room that would be his for the next month. His attention returned to the email he was drafting to the Washington-based podiatric surgeon travelling to Australia to work with his father. As he perused her résumé to find an email address, he couldn't help but notice her impressive qualifications and certifications. A quizzical frown dressed his brow as he wondered why she had chosen to relocate to Adelaide and consult at his father's practice. Then he dropped that line of thought. It was not his concern.

'I hope you don't mind the last-minute change in plans, Dr Phoebe Johnson,' he muttered as he pressed 'send' on the keyboard, hoping that even if she had turned off her computer she would receive the notification via her mobile phone. 'It looks like you'll be working with me not my father. At least until he's back on his feet again.'

Phoebe Johnson had switched off her cell phone an hour earlier. There was no point in having it on as there was only one person who would try to reach her and she would go to any lengths to avoid another conversation with her mother.

Unfortunately her mother had found her.

'Why on earth are you leaving Washington? It's been over three months since you postponed the wedding, Phoebe. It's time you set a new date.'

'I *cancelled* the wedding, Mother. I didn't postpone it.'

Completely dumbfounded, and shaking her head, Phoebe stood on the steps of her rented brownstone apartment, her online printed boarding pass and her passport both gripped in one leather-gloved hand while the other searched for keys in her oversized handbag. The second of her matching tweed suitcases was balanced precariously by her feet, and her heavy woollen coat was buttoned up against the icy December wind that was howling down the narrow car-lined street.

She found her keys and, aware that the meter was running on the double-parked cab, hurriedly locked the front door. She was in no mood for another confrontation and frustrated that at the eleventh hour it was happening again. Her mind was made up. She was not looking back.

'How can you work things out if you go rushing off to another country? Surely you've punished Giles enough for his indiscretion?' her mother continued, not at all deterred by anything Phoebe had said, nor by her imminent travel plans. 'I'm certain he's learnt his lesson.'

Phoebe tugged down her knitted hat, at risk of blowing away in a chilly gust, then made her way down the snow-speckled steps with her last suitcase and handed it to the cab driver, who had been tapping his foot impatiently on the kerb.

'It isn't a punishment, Mother. I ended it. I gave the ring back, returned the wedding presents and told Giles that I never want to see him again. It's about as final as it gets. And I've thought this through until I've gone almost mad. You don't seem to understand—I no longer love Giles and I don't want to see him again. *Ever.* To be honest, I'm surprised that after everything he's put me through you'd want him to have any part in my life.'

She paused as she looked long and hard at her mother, completely bemused that they saw the situation so very differently.

'He's not the man for me. I don't know if there even *is* a man for me, but right now I'm not looking. I want to put all my energy into my work and I refuse to waste another second on Giles.'

With that said, Phoebe headed to the waiting cab. The

headlights of the oncoming traffic were reflected on the icy road as night began to fall.

'That seems so harsh. He really does regret his behaviour. His mother told me so over our bridge game yesterday,' her mother continued as she followed Phoebe, her pace picking up with each step. 'Please see reason, Phoebe. Giles is committed to making it up to you. He's apparently not at all his usual jovial, outgoing self at the moment. He's taken the postponement very seriously. Esme said he's quite sullen, and that's not like him. She thinks he's turned over a new, more responsible leaf. He's sown his last wild oat.'

She placed her gloved hand over Phoebe's as her daughter reached for the door handle of the cab. Stepping closer, she dropped her voice almost to a whisper.

'Darling, you could do worse. Giles is so very handsome—and let's not forget his family tree. His ancestors arrived on the *Mayflower*.'

Phoebe rolled her eyes in horror that her perfectly coiffed mother, dressed in her favourite New York designer's latest winter collection, was pulling out both the looks *and* the ancestry cards. She watched the driver close the trunk, walk to his door and climb inside.

Pulling her hand free, she responded in an equally low voice. 'Let me see… My sulking but extremely good-looking ex-fiancé, with his impeccable lineage, is apparently committed to me but isn't averse to sleeping with other women. Please, Mother, let's not try to paint him as something he isn't. I don't think he is capable of loving anyone but himself, and I don't believe for a minute that he's turned over a new leaf. And, frankly, I don't care. He ruined any chance of us being husband and wife when he chose to cheat on me.'

She kissed her mother goodbye and climbed into the

cab, then dropped the window to hear the last of her mother's not so wise words.

'Darling, as your grandmother always said, every man is entitled to one big mistake in life.'

'He slept with both of my bridesmaids the weekend before our wedding—that's not one big mistake...that's two enormous, deal-breaking mistakes!' Phoebe's voice was no longer soft or controlled and she didn't mind if the cab driver heard. Her frustration had limited her ability to care.

'If you want to be *technical*, it's two....but couldn't you see fit to consider it Giles's one weekend of poor judgement and call it the same mistake?'

The cab pulled away and Phoebe slumped back into the cold leather seat. Over the rattling of the engine she heard her mother's parting words.

'Darling, don't forget—Christmas is a time for forgiveness.'

Phoebe was abruptly stirred from her unpleasant recollection of the pointless argument that had occurred less than twenty-four hours previously. An impeccably groomed flight attendant was standing beside her seat, accompanied by a young girl in a lime-green sweater and matching pants, with a mass of golden curls, a red headband and a big smile. Everything about her was a little too bright for Phoebe at the end of a long-haul flight.

The little helper reached across to Phoebe with a basket of cellophane-wrapped candy. 'If you chew something it will stop your ears getting blocked when we land. Would you like one?'

Phoebe wasn't sure what she wanted, but politely smiled and accepted a sweet. She would never hurt a child's feelings. She had no idea what Phoebe had been put through, and she envied her innocence just a little. The young girl had no idea that boys grew into cads.

'Thank you,' she said, and as the pair moved on to the next passenger Phoebe unwrapped the candy and slipped it into her mouth.

She wasn't sure of anything. She should be a happily married woman back from an eight-week honeymoon in Europe, but instead she was a single woman about to arrive in the land Down Under. And this trip was probably the first of many she would make on her own.

Midway over the Pacific Ocean she had looked out of her tiny window into complete darkness. It had represented her life...the huge unknown.

The very thought of ever trusting a man again was ludicrous. She would more than likely see out her days as a spinster, she'd told herself as she had flicked through the choices of inflight entertainment when the rest of the passengers had been sound asleep. Her head had been much too busy thinking about things that she knew she couldn't change, and her thoughts had been as unrelenting as they'd been painful.

All men were the same—well, except for her father, she had reminded herself, as she'd realised there was nothing she'd wanted to watch on her personal screen and pulled down her satin night mask to try and shut out the world. He was one of the last decent men and then they broke the mould.

Susy, her best friend since junior college, who had left Washington two years previously to work as a barrister for the Crown Prosecution Service in London, agreed with her. She had sworn off relationships after her last disastrous rendezvous three months prior.

Men were not worth the effort or the heartbreak, the two friends had decided over a late-night international call before Phoebe's flight. They'd both eaten copious amounts of ice cream in different time zones as they'd commiserated. Susy had been devouring her feel-good salted caramel treat after returning home from a long day in court, while Phoebe had been scraping the melted remnants of her cookies and cream ice cream at just past midnight, Washington time.

'They're just not worth it,' Susy had said into the phone as she'd dropped her empty bowl and spoon on the coffee table, kicked off her shoes and reached for a throw.

'Absolutely not worth even a second of our time,' Phoebe had agreed. 'They are full of baloney—and I'm not talking about the good Italian mortadella. I'm talking the cheap and nasty supermarket kind of baloney.'

'My sentiments exactly.'

'Men and women shouldn't even be on the same planet.'

'Not even the same universe,' Susy had replied, reaching for the bowl of luxury candies her mother had sent over for her recent birthday. She'd still been suffering from post-break-up sugar cravings. 'I think the entire male race should be banished. Except for your dad, though, Phoebs—John's a real sweetie, so he can stay. Mine hasn't called since my birthday, so he can take a jet to another planet for a while with the rest of them.'

Not long after their decision to relocate the earth's male population Phoebe had felt her eyes getting heavy and had said goodnight to her friend. She was glad she had such a wonderful friend, but very sad that they had both been hurt by callous men. She had no clue why they had both been dealt bad men cards, but she was resolute that it would never happen again.

Because neither of them would ever date again.

From that day forward it would be all about their careers.

The plane dropped altitude to land. The sun was up and Phoebe looked from the window to see varied-sized squares of brown and green crops making a patchwork quilt of the undulating landscape. It was nothing like landing in Washington, where she lived, or New York, where she had undertaken her medical studies. Australia couldn't be further from either, in distance or in landscape, and for that reason she couldn't be more relieved.

She was a little anxious, but she was a big girl, she kept reminding herself. It would be a healing adventure. A time to bury the past and focus on furthering her career in podiatric surgery. And time away from her mother. As much as Phoebe loved her, she doubted she would miss her while she was still clearly on Team Giles.

Phoebe did, however, have a strong bond with her father John, and would miss him and their long chats about local and world politics, theology, and to which particular rat species Giles belonged. Susy was right—her father *was* one of the last good men. Over the years he had taught Phoebe to seek out answers, to find her path and not to be afraid to experience life and the joys the world had to offer. He had told her always to demand in return the same good manners and consideration that she gave to others, and most importantly to smile…even if her heart was breaking. There were always others far worse off.

And, much to the chagrin of his wife, John had agreed that time away from Washington and the wedding debacle was the best idea for Phoebe.

'We are now commencing our descent into Adelaide. Please ensure your tray table is secured and your seat is in the upright position. We will be landing in fifteen minutes and you will be disembarking at gate twenty-three. The current time in Adelaide is eleven-thirty. Your luggage will be available for collection on Carousel Five. Adelaide is experiencing a heatwave and expecting an extremely hot forty-three degrees for the fifth day in a row. For our overseas passengers, that's a hundred and nine degrees Fahrenheit—so shorts and T-shirts would be the order of the week, since the hot spell is not ending for another few days! We hope you enjoyed your flight and will choose to fly with us in the future.'

Phoebe rested back in her seat and her mind drifted back to the snow-covered streets of Washington that she had left behind. And to her cheating fiancé and quite possibly the world's worst bridesmaids... She thought of her position at the university hospital...and of how, after the flight attendant's announcement, she might quite possibly die of heat stroke on her first day in a new country...

Fifteen minutes later, a disembarked and ever so slightly dishevelled Phoebe looked around the sea of strangers waiting with her in line at Customs and questioned herself for heading to a country where she didn't know a soul. But then reason reminded her that the alternative would be crazier.

Staying with the very charismatic but totally insincere Giles. Accepting his pathetic 'last fling' excuse and her mother's unrelenting need to defend his abominable behaviour due to his impressive family tree... Giles's womanising would have his notable ancestors with their seventeenth-century Pilgrim morals turning in their graves.

She shook her head as she moved one step closer to the booth where a stern-looking official was scrutinising the passports of the very weary long-haul travellers wanting to enter the country.

Despite her stomach churning with nerves at the prospect of being so far from home, particularly at Christmas, she knew she had done the right thing. Remaining in her home town wasn't an option as the two families were joined at the hip, and that closeness wasn't allowing her to heal and move on. Thanksgiving had gone a long way to proving her right, with both families and a supposedly contrite Giles gathering and expecting her to join them. She'd refused, but she had known immediately that Christmas gatherings would be no different.

If she'd stayed it would have given her mother a glimmer of hope that she would rekindle her relationship with Giles. That an ensuing wedding of the year in Washington might be on the cards again, and that the wedding planner would once again ask Phoebe's father to check the diary of the Vice-President to ensure he could attend.

In Phoebe's mind there was absolutely no chance that she would wed a man who had been unfaithful. She couldn't turn the other cheek and ignore his indiscretions. It was the twenty-first century and she had choices. She wanted to be a man's equal partner in life. That was what she needed and if she never found it then she would not take second best. She would rather spend her life alone.

For better or worse with Giles would mean Phoebe always hoping his behaviour would get better, but knowing he'd more than likely get worse. The further away she stepped from her ex-fiancé the more she suspected he had done her a huge favour by showing his true nature before the wedding. No doubt, she surmised, having a wife who wouldn't ruffle feathers but would instead add value to his reputation by having her own medical career, and whose father was a Presidential advisor, had all been part of Giles' political game plan.

It had become painfully clear once she'd broken up with him that Giles had manipulated her for his own benefit. She thought she had fallen in love, but now she wasn't so sure. Perhaps it had been a little rushed, and she'd been caught up in the idea of happily-ever-after once the wedding momentum had started. All of her friends except for Susy were engaged or married and it had seemed a natural progression.

The wedding had been set up so quickly by her mother who, along with Washington's most popular wedding planner, had had everything moving at the speed of light.

Susy had accepted the role of her maid of honour, and the two young women had been excited about seeing each other after so long, but the day before she'd been due to fly out Susy had called and broken disappointing news. She was unable to leave London as the jury had not returned the verdict on a very prolonged case. In her own words, she'd said she'd have to miss the wedding of her best friend in the world in order to see some bad guys locked away for a very long time in an English prison.

Deflated and disappointed, Phoebe had understood, but it had left her with only two distant cousins in her bridal party. She had agreed to include the young women, who were both twice removed on her mother's side of the family, because she had been secure in the knowledge that Susy would be beside her for the days leading up to her wedding and with her at the altar of the Cathedral Church of Saint Peter and Saint Paul.

She barely knew the girls. She hadn't seen them in over five years and from what she had heard they were party girls who were living on the west coast and their antics in social media were a constant source of embarrassment to their respective families.

It had been decided that it was time they returned to Washington and settled down. They were both single and in their early twenties, and the families' combined strategy had been to use the wedding as their wayward daughters' entrée into the right circles. They'd hoped that a society wedding would help the girls meet potential husbands and leave their wild life behind them.

Unfortunately that had never happened. They'd flown in a few days before the final dress fittings and managed to ruin Phoebe's life in the process.

Looking back, Phoebe realised that everything about that day had been wrong, but at the time she hadn't been able to step back far enough to see it for what it really was. But now she could. The three months since the scheduled wedding day that never happened had given her time to see Giles for the man he was. Controlling, calculating and ambitious. There was nothing wrong with ambition, but, fuelled by his other character flaws and good looks, it made for a man who would do whatever he wanted, whenever he wanted—and apparently with whomever he wanted. A misogynist, with a lot of family money and connections.

Phoebe would be eternally grateful to the best man, Adrian, who had delivered the bad news the day before their nuptials. She appreciated that it had been a difficult call for him, but knew he had spent a number of months working closely as a political intern with her father and respected him enormously. Adrian had told Phoebe that he cared too much for her and her family to stand by and let Giles hurt her. He'd broken the boys' club rules and she knew he would no doubt pay the price with his peers. She also knew that her father would do his best to support him, but Adrian was not motivated by professional gain and that made his act even more admirable. Honesty in the political arena was rare, and Phoebe and her father were both grateful.

Phoebe's head was spinning as she was finally called up to one of the immigration booths. She dragged her hand luggage behind her and handed over her passport. Then, with everything in order, her visa was stamped and she was waved through to collect her luggage.

'Enjoy your stay, Miss Johnson.'

Phoebe's lips curved slightly. It was an attempt at a smile but she was still not sure how she felt and whether she had just made another of life's bad calls—a huge error she would live to regret almost as much as accepting the first date with Giles and, six short months later, his proposal in the opulent wood-panelled and chandelier-filled dining room of that five star hotel in Washington.

The ring was a spectacular four-carat diamond, set in platinum, and it had been served on a silver platter alongside her *crème brûlée* dessert. A single strategically placed violin had played as Giles had fallen to one knee. But it had only been a fleeting kiss on the forehead he'd given her when she'd agreed to be his wife.

It hadn't been a passionate relationship, but she had still believed their life together could be perfect. He wasn't one to show public displays of affection and she had accepted that. In hindsight, she suspected he preferred to look around at all the enamoured faces in the room rather than at hers. He had enjoyed the attention the proposal had focused on him. In person and in the media.

As she shuffled through the airport to collect her checked baggage Phoebe drew a deep breath and thought about the irony of his reticence in showing any public display of affection with her while enjoying very *private* displays of affection with other women. And she felt sure there had been more than the two she knew about. It was all about appearances. And what happened behind closed doors seemed inconsequential to him.

She shuddered with the thought of how close she'd come to being his wife. And the lies that would have been the foundation of their marriage.

No matter what lay ahead, her life *had* to be better than that.

## CHAPTER TWO

THE MOMENT PHOEBE saw the sign *'Welcome to Adelaide'* she decided she would quiet her doubts. There was no room for second-guessing herself. She was already in her new home. *This is it,* she said to herself silently as she collected her luggage and then made her way to the cab rank. *No turning back now.*

The airport was only twenty minutes from the centre of town, where she would be living. The town she would call home for six months. Six months in which she hoped to sort out her life, her head, and if possible her heart—and forget about the man who had seduced her bridesmaids.

'You were supposed to meet potential husbands—not hump the groom!' she muttered under her breath.

Phoebe noticed the cab driver staring at her strangely in the rear vision mirror. His eyes widened. She realised that her muttering must have been audible to him and she bit her lip and looked out of the window in silence.

Phoebe paid the driver, giving him a generous tip. She had been told it was not necessary in Australia, but it was second nature. He placed her suitcases on the pavement and tucked the fare into his pocket. She was left standing in the heat.

It was a dry heat, like the Nevada desert, and it engulfed her like a hot blanket dropped from the sky. She was grateful that she had changed on the two-hour stopover in Auckland, and was now wearing a light cotton sundress and flat sandals. She lugged her heavy suitcases, one at a time, up the steps to the quaint single-fronted sandstone townhouse that she prayed had air-conditioning. The suitcases were so heavy it would have cost a small fortune in excess baggage if her father hadn't insisted on paying for her first class flight.

On Phoebe's personal budget, post hand-beaded wedding dress, along with the purchase of the maid of honour's and the bridesmaids' dresses, beautifully crafted designer heels for four, three pearl thank-you bracelets and half of a non-refundable European honeymoon, she could only have managed a premium economy flight. But she'd been so desperate to leave Washington for the furthest place that came to mind she would have rowed to Australia just to get away from the drama of the cancelled wedding and her desolate mother.

Phoebe drew another laboured breath. A week ago she'd known little of Adelaide, save the international bike race and the tennis that took over the city in January. Her career as a podiatric surgeon specialising in sports-related conditions made her aware of most large-scale sporting events worldwide. She hoped that her skills would be utilised in Adelaide, a city ten thousand miles from home. She was there with no clear plan for the future. She did, however, have a job.

Her father had been wonderful. It was fortunate for Phoebe that his role at the White House gave him the knowledge and connections to assist her, which meant that her application to practise in Australia had been fast-tracked. She met all of the criteria, and her credentials were impeccable, so approval had been granted.

She'd had the option of a small practice in Adelaide

or a much larger practice in Melbourne that focused entirely on elite sportsmen and women. While the second option was her dream job, it was still a few weeks off being secured, and Phoebe had liked the idea of leaving town immediately. She had also done some research around the sole practitioner, Dr Ken Rollins, a podiatric surgeon in his early sixties with an inner-city practice and the need for an associate for six months. The position sounded perfect. His research papers were particularly interesting and Phoebe looked forward to working with him.

So she was more than happy with her decision. They were two very different opportunities, but she felt confident she had made the right choice.

Opening the door to her leased townhouse was heavenly. It was like opening a refrigerator. The air-conditioning was on high and the blinds were half closed, giving a calm ambience to the space. There was a large basket of fruit and assorted nibbles on the kitchen bench. Her father, no doubt, she mused.

She dropped her bags, closed the front door and wandered around the house for a moment before she found the bedroom and flung herself across the bed. Embarrassed at remembering what she'd said to herself in the cab, she kicked off her shoes and then reminded herself that the driver would have witnessed far worse than a jet-lagged passenger's mutterings. The pillow was so cool and soft against her face as she closed her heavy eyes. Exhaustion finally got the better of her and she fell into a deep unexpected sleep.

It was nearly four hours before Phoebe stirred from her unplanned afternoon nap. Her rumbling stomach had woken her and she remembered the basket she had spied on her arrival. The fruit was delicious, and she had opened the refrigerator door to find sparkling water, assorted juices, a cold seafood platter, two small salads and half a dozen single serve yoghurt tubs.

*Thanks, Dad.*

She smiled. She knew her father must have called the landlord and arranged for the house to be stocked. She knew, despite what she said, that he felt to blame for the way everything had turned out as *he* had introduced to her young, 'going places' political intern fiancé.

John Johnson had thought Giles was a focussed young man with a huge career ahead of him and he'd had no hesitation in introducing him to Phoebe. He'd been polite, astute, with no apparent skeletons in the closet, and from a well-respected Washington family. But they had all been hoodwinked.

There was no way that John could have foreseen the disaster. And he had done everything in his power to get her away from the situation when it had turned ugly. Phoebe would never blame him for anything.

After eating, Phoebe showered and sent her father a text message to let him know she was safe and sound and to thank him for everything he had arranged. Then she raised the air-conditioning temperature enough to ensure that she didn't freeze during the night before setting the alarm on her phone and climbing back into bed.

She just wanted to be fresh and not suffering the effects of jet-lag.

Eight hours later, as Phoebe lifted the blinds and looked across the Adelaide parklands, she felt refreshed. She had never flown such a distance and had expected to be exhausted, but she was feeling better than she had in months. It was as if a weight had been lifted from her shoulders.

The view from her bedroom window was picturesque. The morning sun lit up the large pinkish-grey gum trees towering over the beautifully manicured gardens. The flowers were in bloom in the garden's beds and it was like a pastel rainbow. It was a new beginning.

She reached for her phone and took a snapshot, sent it to her father in a quick text, then headed for the shower. She wasn't about to be late for her first day on the job. She wanted to get there early and learn the ropes before the patients arrived. Working with an older, more experienced specialist would be a learning experience for Phoebe, and she was excited by the prospect. It would keep her mind off everything she had been through.

Ken Rollins's papers focussed on his holistic and conservative approach in treating lower limb conditions, using a variety of modalities such as gait retraining, orthotic therapy, dry needling and exercise modification. Phoebe had printed the most recent before she'd left Washington and she'd read it on her flight over. He would be a great mentor.

It was going to be a much-needed change and Phoebe couldn't be more optimistic. After all, she had heard Adelaide was the place to raise children or retire, and it had the highest aging population of any other capital city, so she assumed there would be a lower than average population of single men. Single, arrogant, self-serving men, all incapable of remaining faithful. There truly couldn't be a better city in the world for her at that moment, but for the fact that she knew she would miss Christmas with her family. It was her favourite time of year. But it was the price she had to pay for her sanity.

As Phoebe stepped out of her house half an hour later the heat of the day was already building. She felt glad she had chosen a simple cream skirt that skimmed her knees, a black and cream striped blouse and black patent Mary Jane kitten heels with a slingback, so she didn't need to wear stockings. Her shoulder-length chestnut hair was pulled into a high ponytail and she had applied tinted sunscreen, a light lip gloss and some mascara.

She hoped the practice rooms would be as cool as her townhouse. Her previous address at this time of the year was freezing cold at best and icy on bad days. She knew she wouldn't cope in the heat for too long, but felt confident that the inner-city practice would be cool as a cucumber.

Unfortunately, as she discovered five minutes later, she couldn't have been more wrong. The air-conditioning at the practice had been working overtime during the heatwave. Phoebe had arrived when the city had been sweltering for close to a week. The infrastructure of the old building was buckling and clearly the air-conditioning had been the first thing to succumb. It was like a sauna as she entered, and she wondered if it wasn't cooler outside than inside the old building.

A bell above the door had chimed as she'd walked in but the waiting room was empty and it appeared no one had heard her enter. Standing alone in the uncomfortable, stifling air she felt sure that in minutes she would be reduced to a melting mess. Not a great first impression, she surmised as she looked around anxiously, all the while hoping that Ken Rollins would appear at any minute and take her into the air-conditioned section of the practice. There *had* to be an air-conditioned part.

Then, in the distance, she heard a noise and saw a very tall male figure walking down the corridor towards her. She blinked as she saw that he was bare to the waist with a white hand towel around his neck. She pinned her hopes on the fact this man was working on the air-conditioning and that he was good at his job, because she was wilting quickly. And she doubted her more senior boss would enjoy working in these conditions either.

She couldn't help but notice as he drew near that the man was wearing dress pants and highly polished shoes. Although nothing covered his very chiselled, sweat-dampened chest.

'I'm looking for Dr Ken Rollins. I'm Dr Phoebe Johnson from Washington.'

'*You're* Phoebe Johnson?' the man said, with a look of surprise on his handsome face and doubt colouring his deep voice.

'Yes, I am. Did he tell you I was arriving?'

The man wiped his forehead and then his hands on the towel he was carrying, then stretched out his free hand. 'I'm Heath Rollins, Ken's son, and I've been expecting you.'

His voice was sonorous and austere. And the frown on Phoebe's face did little to mask her confusion. *Why on earth was he expecting her and why was he half naked?*

'So are you here to repair the air-conditioning for your father?'

'Not exactly. I'm attempting to repair the air-con, but I'm not a repairman—not even close as you can tell by how hot it still is in here. I'm a podiatric surgeon from Sydney.'

Phoebe was more confused than ever. Why did Ken Rollins have his *podiatric surgeon* son trying to fix the air-conditioning unit? And why wasn't Ken there to meet her?

'Is your father in with patients already?' she asked as she looked around her surroundings, hoping that the older surgeon would suddenly appear and clear up the confusion. And bring his son a shirt so he could cover up.

'No, he's not…'

'Is he running late?'

'No he's not,' he replied without any hint of emotion in his reply. 'I'm actually standing in for him for the next four weeks.'

Phoebe quickly realised as she shook his hand that the man standing before her was potentially her new boss. She took a few steps back from the very warm handshake and looked warily at him. She had signed on to work with *Ken* Rollins. *This* Dr Rollins was definitely not in his sixties. *Disastrous*, was the first thought that came to her mind. The second thought, as she looked at his lightly tanned physique, was not in any way ladylike and nothing she wanted to be considering with this man. Or *any* man, now that she had sworn off the species. It was not what she needed. In fact this was close to a catastrophe.

She had envisaged an older, established and experienced mentor to work closely with for five days a week over the next six months. This was supposed to be a professional development opportunity. And the man standing before her stripped to the waist was anything but professional development. He was not what she wanted and nor did she have the capacity to deal with him either. With the combination of Heath Rollins's half-naked physique and the heat in the room Phoebe knew she had stepped into the fire—literally.

'Where exactly *is* your father?' she asked. 'And why are you stepping in for him?'

As she spoke she was doing her best not to be distracted by his very toned body or his equally gorgeous eyes. But it was a struggle, and she faced the prospect that the cruel hand of the universe had just replaced her playboy fiancé with someone even more handsome, if a comparison was to be made. And she had to work with him until almost the middle of the following year. Six long months.

She settled her eyes on the stubble-covered cleft in his chin, then moved them to his soft full lips, framed by dimples and slightly smiling, and then finally she looked up and discovered his brilliant blue eyes.

She had to admit that he was a very different type from

Giles. This man had more cowboy good-looks, while Giles was the Wall Street slick type. But she didn't want *any* type of good-looking and she was far from happy with the arrangement. Good-looking men were all the same, and a long-haul trip to the other side of the world only to find that fate had ordered her another one was not what she had wanted.

Suddenly she felt a little dizzy. The heat was closing in by the minute. She mopped her forehead with a tissue as she reached for a seat and promptly sat down with a sigh. Her plans had gone terribly awry and the added lack of air-conditioning made it unbearable. This was nothing close to the first day she had planned in her mind.

'I sent you an email outlining the changes,' he said, his lean fingers rubbing his chin. 'You shouldn't be surprised.'

'What email?' she managed as she looked around for something to use as a fan and grabbed a magazine, which she moved frantically through the air in front of her face in the hope that it would cool her down.

'The one that clearly explained my father was in an accident two days ago, fractured his patella and had to undergo surgery, so you'll be working alongside me until he returns.'

'So he's coming back?' she asked, with a little relief colouring her voice. 'When, exactly?'

'In about a month, if his rehabilitation goes as planned. It wasn't a complete reconstruction, so he should be back on deck a lot sooner than after a full recon.'

Phoebe nodded and bit the inside of her cheek as she considered his response. At least it was four weeks, not six months. She felt a little better about the time frame but the confirmation that Heath was going to be her boss, for however short or long a time, was still not news she needed to hear.

She kept her improvised fan moving through the thick air, trying to bring some relief to the situation. Against the oppressive heat it was little use; against news of the working arrangements it was no use at all. For the next four weeks she would be working with a man too handsome for his own good and definitely for the good of all the women who fell victim to his charm. But, thinking of what she had just escaped, she knew she would never fall for a man like Heath. Not that she was on the market for anyone anyway.

She loosened the belt cinched at her waist to allow her to breathe a little more easily in the mugginess that was wrapping around her.

'You're looking extremely pale,' he said, with something she thought sounded like a level of concern. 'I'll get a glass of water for you.'

Phoebe swayed to and fro in her seat, watching as Heath crossed back to her with a plastic cup he had filled from the water cooler. She took a few sips, then shakily handed him back the cup. Just as the polished wooden floor became a checked pattern that surged towards her in waves. As she fought the swirling focus that made her feel more disorientated by the minute, she wondered why any of this had happened to her.

Was there any way she could escape the heat? Why did Ken have to wreck his knee *now*? Why did she have to work with *this* man for the next few weeks?

Suddenly there were no more questions. The stifling heat finally claimed her. And Dr Phoebe Johnson fainted into Heath's strong arms.

# CHAPTER THREE

'GOOD, YOU'RE BACK with us.'

Phoebe heard the deep timbre of a male voice very close, and when she opened her eyes she realised just how close. She was facing some well-defined and very naked male abdominal muscles, only inches away from her. Her brow formed a frown as she realised she recognised the distinctly Australian accent. It was her temporary boss—and in her direct line of vision was his bare tanned stomach.

Still lying down, she attempted to let her eyes roam her surroundings—until she was finally forced to look up and see Heath looking down at her. She couldn't read his expression. He wasn't frowning, but nor was he smiling. His look was serious. Concerned. And the concern appeared genuine. She discovered her resting place was an examination table. And soon realised there was a cool towel on her forehead and that a portable fan was stirring the heavy air and moving the fine wisps of hair that had escaped from her ponytail.

'She's lucky you were there to catch her. Sorry—I stepped out to get a cool drink and missed her.'

Phoebe heard a second voice. It belonged to a female but she couldn't see anyone from her vantage point. It made sense to her, even in her disorientated state, that for him to have set so much in place so quickly, such as the cool towel and the fan, he had to have had some assistance.

'I must apologise, Phoebe. I'd hoped to have the air-con up and running before you arrived,' Heath said, in a serious, professional tone that belied his appearance. He looked more like a private dancer than a stoic doctor. 'I'm not surprised you passed out. Aussie summers can be tough if you're not used to them.'

Phoebe was so embarrassed when she realised what had happened. She stirred from her horizontal position, but still felt light-headed so didn't attempt to sit completely upright immediately. But while she slowly moved she remembered a little of the conversation they had shared—including the news he had imparted to her. *'You'll be working along-side me.'* Silently she begged the universe to tell her it wasn't true.

The last thing she needed was a man like Heath. She needed to be thinking about her career as a podiatric surgeon and she wanted to be taught by an experienced older practitioner. This new arrangement was not a dynamic she had even considered as a possibility when she'd agreed to work in Adelaide. She'd thought it would be six months of respite. An emotionally healing time packaged as a working sabbatical.

'Here's some water,' the young woman said as she stepped into view, and she handed Heath a glass with a plastic concertina straw. 'It's not too cold.'

Phoebe squinted as she tried to focus. The woman looked to be in her mid-twenties. Blonde, quite tall, very pretty, with a lovely smile. Phoebe suddenly felt Heath's strong arm lift her upright, yet there was no warmth in the way he held her. It was as if she was an inanimate object.

'Hold on to your cold compress and sip this,' he said as he curved the straw to meet her lips.

He held the drink steady with one hand while the other still supported her. His bedside manner she would have described as 'reserved' at best.

Phoebe held the cold towel in place as she slowly sucked the water through the straw and felt immediately better for it. But the sight of her skirt no longer demurely skimming her knees did not make her feel good at all. Most of her legs were bare, for the world and Dr Heath Rollins to see, and she was horrified.

'I've had enough, thank you,' she said as she moved her mouth away from the drink and then, struggling to keep the towel on her head, she tried to lift her bottom slightly and release the hem of the skirt.

There was little covered at all. Fainting and baring parts of her anatomy that should be saved for the beach, or more intimate encounters, was definitely *not* a great start to this already less than desirable working relationship. She had secured the job purely on her references, and now she could only guess what he was thinking as she reached down to gain some dignity.

'Here—let me help you.'

His hands lifted her gently and with ease. Her heartbeat suddenly increased with the unexpected touch of his hands on her bare skin. Suddenly she did not feel like an inanimate object. And this time her giddiness wasn't from the heat of the room. His closeness while he held her up made the job of adjusting her clothing difficult. She finally wriggled the skirt into place and swung her legs around, subtly encouraging Heath to release her and step back.

Clearing her throat, and raising her chin a little defensively, Phoebe looked at Heath as if he were almost the perpetrator of the incident. 'How exactly—?' she began and then paused for a moment. 'How did I get here? I don't remember leaving the reception area. I do remember feeling very hot, then light-headed, but where was I when I fainted?'

'You passed out on a chair in the waiting room, and I carried you in here and put you on your side. You were out for less than a minute. As soon as your head was level with your body you came to.'

The way he spoke was quite clinical and detached, but she still managed to feel uneasy at the mental picture of him scooping her up in his arms and carrying her to the examination bed with little or no effort.

Her eyes briefly scanned his firefighter physique before she blinked and turned away. Ken Rollins would be back before she knew it, she told herself. Then all would be right in her world again. This was just a hiccup in her plans. And if Heath's attitude was anything to go by she had nothing to worry about. His body might have been created for sin but his manner certainly hadn't.

'Thank you. I'm sorry I created such a fuss.' Her tone quickly mimicked his coolness.

'These things happen, but you seem fine now,' he said as he stepped back further and turned to face the other woman.

'Tilly, you can finish up. I think we're fine here. Thanks for cancelling the next two days' patients. The air-con should be repaired by Thursday. You can pick up the twins from childcare early and stay home for a couple of days.'

'Are you sure, Heath? I can come in and do some accounts and general office catch-up work tomorrow.'

'No,' he replied firmly, wiping his brow with the back of his hand. 'It's like a sauna today and it will be worse tomorrow. It's a health and safety issue to be working in these conditions.'

'All right—have it your way,' Tilly said as she reached over and kissed him on the cheek. 'See you at home tonight, then. Oh, and Dr Johnson? I hope you feel better soon.'

'Thank you, but please call me Phoebe.'

Phoebe looked down at the young woman's hand as she left the room and saw a wedding band and stunning solitaire diamond. They were married. And they had twins. Of course they did. They were perfect for each other. Two stunning blonde Aussies, sun-kissed and fabulous. She could only guess how gorgeous their children would be.

Phoebe wondered if she had read Heath incorrectly. Perhaps he *wasn't* a Giles clone. Perhaps he was an austere but loving husband who just happened to be very good-looking and in Phoebe's still emotionally raw state that had incorrectly translated to him being a potential cad. All good-looking men had been tarnished by Giles. And she had clearly been scarred.

She suddenly felt very self-conscious, and a little sad at her own ability to jump to conclusions. Perhaps all men were not the same... Just the one she had chosen. And Susy's recent choice too.

Moving awkwardly on the examination table, she tried to inch her skirt down further to cover her knees.

He shook his head. 'You don't have to rush to cover up. I'm not looking at your legs, if that's what you're worried about.'

Phoebe felt instantly embarrassed. She began fidgeting nervously and smoothing the rest of her clothes into place, and then tidying her hair in an attempt to gain composure without saying a word. There was nothing that came to mind that wouldn't make her appear even sillier and more self-conscious, so she stayed silent.

Heath watched the way she was fussing. He found her behaviour so far from the image he had created in his mind of a podiatric surgeon from Washington with impeccable references, who was triple board certified in surgery, orthopaedics, and primary podiatric medicine. She was also a Fellow of the American College of Foot and Ankle Surgeons, the American Academy of Podiatric Sports Medicine and the American College of Foot & Ankle Orthopaedics & Medicine. All of those qualifications had had him picturing someone very different. He'd thought she would be brimming with confidence, more than a little aloof. And definitely nowhere near as pretty.

Dr Phoebe Johnson had taken Heath by surprise...

Phoebe's blood pressure had slowly returned to normal and she felt more steady physically.

'So, what would you like me to do? I guess if you've cancelled the patients there's probably no point me being here. I can take some patient notes back to my house and read over them.'

She looked around and ascertained where she was in relation to the front door and the reception area, where she assumed her bag would be, and headed in that direction. His wife, she assumed, had already left.

'There's definitely no point you staying here, and to be honest your first two days' patients are post-op and quite straightforward,' he told her as he followed her out to where her bag was resting by a chair. 'Here is probably the worst place to be. We don't want a repeat performance.'

The waiting room and reception area was even hotter as it faced the glare of the morning sun on the huge glass panes.

'If you're sure I can't do anything here, then I'll see you on Thursday.'

She reached for the front door and he stepped closer to her to hold the door open. Her face looked angelic, and he was intrigued by her. He momentarily wondered why, with all her experience and qualifications, she wanted to work in Adelaide, of all places? Suddenly he felt curious. She was just nothing like he had imagined. He could work out most people, and he prided himself on being able to know what made them tick. But not her. Not yet.

When he'd glanced over her résumé in search of her contact details he had worried that she would not find the practice enough of a challenge, with her interests and her extensive experience in sports podiatry, but then had conceded that she had made her professional choice and it was none of his concern. And if she did grow bored and move on before the six months were up—again, it was not his concern. He wouldn't be there long enough for it to have any impact on him. His father could find a replacement if she did.

'Okay, I'll see you on Thursday.'

'Yes. I'll see you then,' Phoebe responded as she walked past him into a wall of warm, dry air.

She wasn't sure if it was warmer outside than in, but it felt less humid—although she quickly realised neither was particularly pleasant. It was still early, but the pavement held the heat from the day before and she could tell it would be blisteringly hot in a few hours.

'I hope you find a way to stay cool.'

Without much emotion in his voice, but clearly being polite, he said, 'I think I'll take my son to the pool later on today. Maybe you should hit the beach or a pool—there's quite a few around. There are some indoor ones too. Oscar's looking forward to finding some other children to play with.' Before he turned to walk inside he added, 'I hope you find a way to stay cool too.'

Phoebe stopped in her tracks. 'I thought you and your wife had twins?' she called back to him from the bottom step, with a curious frown dressing her brow.

'No, my sister Tilly has twin girls, but they're only two

and a half years old. Oscar's five,' he told her, with a little more animation. 'Tilly's like a mother to Oscar while we're in town, and it's been good for him since it's just the two of us the rest of the time. I'm sure as they grow up the cousins will all be great friends, but right now Oscar really doesn't find them much fun at all.'

He looked back at Phoebe with an expression she couldn't quite make out as he paused in the doorway, as if he was thinking something through before he spoke.

Phoebe turned to leave.

'It's ridiculously hot out there,' he remarked, catching her attention. 'If you have time perhaps we could pop round to the corner café and grab a cool drink. I wouldn't want you fainting on the way home. I can answer any questions you have about the practice.'

Phoebe could see he was a very serious man—nothing like Giles, with his smooth flirtatious manner. But there was something about Heath that made her curious. She reminded herself that she would never be interested in him in any way romantically, but with his demeanour she didn't flag him as a threat to her reborn virginal status. And she did want to know about the running of the practice so she decided to accept his invitation. He was her boss after all.

'I have time.'

Phoebe had decided on the quick walk to the café that she did not want to discuss her personal life and that she would not enquire about his. She knew enough. He was Ken Rollins's son. He was filling in for a month, and he was the single father of a five-year-old boy. That was more than enough. Whether he was divorced or had never been married was none of her business and immaterial.

She wasn't going to be spending enough time with Heath for his personal life to matter. Four weeks would pass quickly and then he and his son would be gone. She wasn't sure if she would ever even meet the boy. It wasn't as if a medical practice dealing with feet would be the most interesting place for a child to visit, she mused, so their paths might never cross.

'Thank you,' she said as she stepped inside the wonderfully cool and thankfully not too densely populated coffee shop.

'They make a nice iced coffee,' Heath told her as they made their way to a corner table and he placed his laptop containing patient notes beside him. 'It's barista coffee, and they add ice-cold milk and whipped cream. They do it well.'

'Sounds perfect—but perhaps hold the cream.'

'Looking after your heart?' he enquired as he pulled out the chair for her.

*In more ways than one*, she thought.

It was a surprise to Phoebe how easy she found it to talk with Heath. While he was still reserved, and borderline frosty, he was attentive and engaged in their discussion. He asked about her work at the hospital in Washington and their conversation was far from stilted, due to their mutual love of their specialty. With Giles, she had not spoken much about her work as he hadn't seemed to understand it and nor had he wanted to. It had been plain that he wasn't interested and he'd never pretended to care. It had been all about *his* career aspirations and how they could achieve them together.

'I've seen your résumé—it's impressive, but definitely geared towards sports podiatry. My father's practice is predominately general patient load along with the occasional sportsman or woman—not the focus I assume you're accustomed to. How do you think you will adjust to that?'

'Sports podiatry is a passion of mine. I've been work-ing in a fantastic unit within a large teaching hospital, where we offer a full spectrum of services for the athlete—including physical therapy and surgery, with an emphasis on biomechanics. My focus outside of essential surgical intervention was primarily on orthotic treatment directed to correct structural deficiency and muscular imbalance. But in general my goal is to return any patient, regardless of their profession, to their maximum level of function and allow them to re-engage in an active life.'

Heath agreed with all she was saying, but added, 'I understand—I just hope you don't begin to feel that this practice is not what you signed up for.'

'No, I love what I do—and feet are feet, no matter what the owners of them do.'

Heath found her answer amusing, but he didn't smile. He rarely did, and those moments were saved for his son. And there was still that unanswered question…

'So tell me, Phoebe, if you love the hospital back in your hometown, you enjoy your work and your colleagues, why did you want to leave?'

Phoebe nervously took a sip of the icy drink. It was rich and flavoursome, just as good as he had promised…and she was stalling. 'I needed a break from Washington,' she finally responded.

'A Caribbean cruise or skiing in Aspen would have been easier than relocating to the other side of the world. And if you were looking for alternative employers I'm sure there must be loads of options for someone of your calibre in the US. It's a big country.'

'I wanted more than a quick vacation or a new employer. It was time for a sea change.'

'Like I said, there are a lot of places that would fit that

bill on your own continent—and I'm sure with a lot less red tape than it must have taken for you to work Down Under.'

'I suppose,' she said nonchalantly, trying to deflect his interest in her reasons for being there, which did not seem to be abating easily with anything she said.

It wasn't the Spanish Inquisition, but it felt close. Phoebe did not want to go into the details of her failed engagement to Giles. Nor her desperate need to escape from him and her mother to a place neither would find her. And there was no way he would ever hear from her the tale of the bridesmaids from hell bedding the groom. It was all too humiliating. And still too raw.

Heath was her temporary boss and he would be leaving once his father's knee had healed. The less he knew the better. In fact the less everyone in the city knew about her the better.

'Your father's interest in harnessing the power of bio-mechanics and advanced medical technology to challenge convention and his ensuing breakthrough results were huge draw cards for me to come and work with him. And I wanted to know more about his collaborative approach to co-morbidities. Your father wrote a great paper on the subject of the co-operative approach to treating systemic problems.'

Heath sensed there was more, but he took her cue to leave the subject alone. He appreciated she had a right to her privacy on certain matters. Just as he did to his own. And there was no need for him to know too much, he reminded himself, as they would be working together for a relatively short time and then he would be leaving. Theirs would be a brief working relationship. Nothing more.

But, stepping momentarily away from being her very temporary boss, he had to admit Phoebe was undeniably beautiful.

Phoebe shifted awkwardly in her seat, not sure if Heath had accepted her response and they could move on. Unaware that her glass was empty, she casually took another sip through her straw. Suddenly the loudest slurp she had ever heard rang out. To Phoebe's horror, apparently it was the loudest the people at an adjacent table had ever heard too, as they shot her a curious stare.

The sound echoed around the café. Phoebe's eyes rolled with embarrassment. Only half an hour before she had passed out in his arms, revealed far too much of her legs, and now her manners were more befitting a preschooler. She wanted to find an inconspicuous hole and slink inside. Heath had such a serious demeanour she could only imagine what he was thinking. It was, without doubt, the worst first day on the job of anyone—ever.

'I told you they make the best iced coffee. There's never enough in my glass either,' Heath said, his mouth almost forming a smile.

It was the first time, in the hour or so since they'd met, that she had seen him show anything even vaguely like a smile. And it was the most gorgeous almost-smile she had ever seen. Her heart unexpectedly skipped a beat.

Giles would have been mortified, she thought. He would have shot her a glare that told her she had embarrassed him. His body language would have reminded her that it was unladylike without saying a word. She would have felt his displeasure while those around would have had no idea. But Heath didn't appear to react that way, and it surprised her. Apparently in his eyes it was *not* cringeworthy behaviour—or if he thought it was he certainly masked it well.

She felt her embarrassment slowly dissipate. Maybe it wasn't the worst day ever after all. And that was confirmed when he continued the conversation as if nothing had happened.

'So, how do you see this working arrangement? Are you happy to split your time with taking half of my father's post-operative patients and the remainder to be new patients, along with a surgical roster?'

'That sounds great to me. I'm fairly flexible—not a hard and fast rules kind of woman—so we can just see how it all works out, and if we need to move around within those parameters we can discuss it as it unfolds.'

Heath didn't feel the same way at all. 'You'll learn quickly that I'm a rules kind of a man. I live by a number of them, and if I set something up then I like to stick by it. So I'd rather we made up our minds and set up now the way it will play out.'

'I guess...' Phoebe replied, a little taken aback by his rigid stance on their working arrangements. She had heard that Australian people were laid-back. Heath didn't fit that bill at all. 'But in my opinion most situations have both a teething period and a grey area. There's generally room to manoeuvre and move around with some degree of compromise if you're willing to look for it.'

'Not with me. Once I've made a decision, it's rare that I'll shift my viewpoint. In fact it would take something extraordinary to make me change my mind.'

While she appreciated Heath's honesty upfront, she thought she would pity whoever lived with him if they got the bathroom roster wrong. 'Well, then, since it's only for a month let's go with your way. You undoubtedly know the practice and the patient load better than I do, so I'm happy to carve it in stone right now if that's how it's done around here.'

Heath appreciated her wit, but made no retort.

An hour later they were still at the café. Once they had agreed to their working arrangements Heath had dropped all other lines of questioning and given Phoebe the low-down on the city she would call home for a few months.

Despite the ease with which they spoke, Heath had still not had his questions answered about Phoebe's motives for relocating. But he did know she was a lot more adaptable than he was. It made him curious, although he didn't verbalise it.

With her academic record the surgical world was quite literally her oyster. There would be few, if any, practices or teaching facilities that would not welcome her into their fold with open arms. There was no ring on her finger, but he would not be arrogant enough to assume that there was no man in her life. If there was then he too must be as adaptable as Phoebe, and willing to compromise and let her travel to the other side of the world for work. *He* was not that type of man.

'Adelaide is very quiet, I assume?' she asked as she relaxed back into her chair and admired the artwork on the café walls.

'Yes—a little too relaxed in pace for me. It's very different from Sydney, which I prefer. I grew up here, but moved to Sydney about ten years ago when I finished my internship. I was offered a position on the east coast and I took it.'

'I'd like to see Sydney one day, but I think Adelaide will be lovely for the next six months.'

'Adelaide's like a very large country town,' Heath replied. 'And that's the reason I never stay too long.'

'A large country town suits me. It isn't the size of the town but more the attitude of the people that matters.'

Heath watched Phoebe as she studied the eclectic collection of watercolour paintings and charcoal sketches on the wall. She was smiling as she looked at the work of novice artists and he could see her appreciation of the pieces. There was no sign of the big town superiority that he had thought she might display, and she didn't launch into a spiel about comparisons with Washington, as he had expected.

'That's what my father keeps telling me when I try to get him to relocate to Sydney. He won't budge. He likes the growing medical research sector in Adelaide, even if it's a small city by comparison.'

'From all reports he's one of the finest podiatric surgeons in the southern hemisphere. I look forward to meeting him when he's up to it.' While Heath had not enquired more about her reasons for relocating, to cement that line of questioning shut she added, 'Your father's work is revolutionary in its simplicity, and I respect his conservative approach of proceeding, where possible, with surgery as the second not the first option. His expertise in soft tissue manipulation and trigger point therapy is impressive. A lot of practitioners routinely go for surgery, but your father is quite the opposite, preferring to view his patients through a holistic filter and follow a slightly more protracted but less invasive treatment plan.'

Heath could see that his father's work had made quite an impression on Phoebe. 'I hope you're not disappointed that you'll be working with me. It's like ordering Chinese takeout and having pizza arrive on your doorstep.'

Phoebe liked his quirky analogy, although it seemed at odds with his less than lighthearted nature. He was far from a poor second, and she silently admitted that pizza was a favourite of hers. Heath was charming and knowledgeable, and his reserved demeanour was a pleasant change.

Although his rigid viewpoint might possibly test her reserves of patience in the long term, she was very much looking forward to working with him in the short term.

She doubted he would disappoint on any level, but professional was the only level she was interested in exploring.

Heath considered the woman sitting opposite him for a moment. She was a highly regarded surgeon in their mutual field, but there was a mixture of strength and frailty to her. It was as if she was hiding, or running away from something. And he wasn't sure *why* he wanted to work her out, except that it was as if she was second-guessing herself on some level. He had no idea why she would.

Heath knew that she was an only child, that her father was a Presidential advisor and her mother a Washington socialite, and that she'd spent her high school years at a prestigious private school in Washington. She had openly chatted about that. He also knew that she had graduated top of her class from her studies at the New York College of Podiatric Medicine, and had done her three-year residency at the university hospital.

It would appear she had the makings of someone who could be quite consumed with their own self-importance, but she wasn't. She was, he'd realised quickly, very humble—because Heath knew of her Dux status from his father, not from her. Phoebe hadn't brought it up. It was a huge honour and she was omitting it from her abbreviated life story over morning coffee.

In that way she was not unlike his wife, Natasha—a former model and fashion designer who had also been very humble about the accolades she'd been given both on and off the runway.

Natasha had not been at all what Heath had imagined a model would be like the night he'd met her at a fundraising event. He'd been thirty and she only twenty-three. After a whirlwind courtship they'd married, and Natasha had fallen pregnant soon afterwards. They'd both been so excited and looking forward to growing their family.

Heath had come to learn that she worked actively and tirelessly for many causes—including one to support research into a cure for the disease that had eventually claimed her life. And from that day, Heath's purpose in life—his only focus outside of his work—had been raising their beautiful little boy, Oscar, who had been given life by the only woman Heath had ever loved.

And nothing and no one would ever come between them.

Not his work and not a woman.

It was a promise he'd made to himself five years earlier. The day he lost his wife. The day he'd walked away from the hospital without her and realised he would never again hold her in his arms or wake next to her in the bed they had shared. He'd vowed that day that he would dedicate his life to being the kind of father to their son that Natasha would have wanted.

And he would never wake with another woman in his arms.

He had been true to both promises.

Oddly, sitting with Phoebe, he felt almost comfortable, more at ease than in a long time, and he suspected their mutual professional interests had a lot to do with that. He couldn't remember the last time he had spoken in depth to a woman about his chosen career and engaged in a meaningful conversation. He had taken lovers over the years, but nothing more than a shared night. He left before dawn, and conversation was at the bottom of the list of his needs on those occasions.

'I'd better let you go and I'll head back to the practice and sort out the air-con, or we'll have melted patients for the next few months,' Heath told her in a matter-of-fact tone as he stood. 'It's only December, and both January and February are hotter months in general.'

Phoebe was taken aback by the way Heath ended their time together. He had invited her to go for a drink and now he was excusing himself quite abruptly. Not that she minded at all. In fact she was relieved, as it gave him no further opportunity to quiz her about her personal life.

'You mean hotter than this?' Phoebe asked.

'Not hotter, but hot for longer stretches.'

Phoebe shrugged. 'Well, then, I *really* hope you get the air-conditioner working.'

He paid the tab and walked Phoebe to the door and then out into the street. His body language was stiff and distant again. Any hint of being relaxed had evaporated.

'I'll see you in a few days. Take some downtime to recover from your trip and I'll see you on Thursday morning at eight. If you get a chance, try to head to the beach or a pool. It will do you the world of good.'

Phoebe nodded. 'Okay, thanks—maybe I will.' She walked away, then suddenly turned around and called out. 'Heath, we never discussed Thursday's patients.'

Heath turned back and looked at Phoebe for the longest moment, then glanced at the laptop tucked loosely under his arm. 'We didn't, didn't we?'

# CHAPTER FOUR

'Daddy!'

Heath was welcomed home by tiny arms that wrapped around his knees and hugged him ferociously. He bent down and returned the hug before he picked up his son in his strong arms and swung him around like a carousel ride. Oscar was his reason for living. He had been the beacon of hope during his darkest days. Heath would never let Oscar down. No matter what the future held, he would be his son's anchor through life. He was the only thing that brought a smile to Heath's face and love to an otherwise broken heart.

'How's my favourite little man?' he asked, kissing his tiny son's chubby cheek.

'I'm good, Daddy.'

Heath lowered him to the ground, then sat on the sofa. Oscar climbed up next to him.

'Can we go to the pool tomorrow—can we, please?'

Heath considered his son for a moment. He had his mother's deep brown eyes and he was the apple of his father's. There was nothing Heath wouldn't do for him, but he did like to have fun and tease him a little sometimes.

'I thought you hated the pool? You distinctly told me the other day that you never, *ever* wanted to go swimming again. You said that you would rather eat live worms than go to a swimming pool!'

'Don't be silly, Daddy. I *loooooove* the pool!'

Heath picked Oscar up and put him on his lap and held him tightly. 'Then it looks like tomorrow we're off to the pool, my little man.'

Phoebe enjoyed a lazy sleep-in the next day. It would end, she knew, when the air-conditioning at the practice was repaired, so she made the most of it. Then she had a quick shower, put on shorts, sandals and a T-shirt, and went out to buy a newspaper. While she enjoyed a light breakfast she planned on reading local stories of interest and about the issues affecting the town she would call home for the near future.

When she arrived home there was a delivery man on her doorstep, holding a medium-sized box, which she signed for and carried into the kitchen.

She discovered it was filled with Christmas gifts. All wrapped in colourful paper and equally pretty ribbons. And every one had her name on it.

She rang her father, but it went to voicemail. 'Hi, Dad. I know you're probably busy, but thank you so much for my gifts. By the way, how did you get the presents here the very day after I arrived?'

A few minutes later, as she was putting the presents away in her wardrobe, she received a text message.

I posted them a week before you left. Hope you like them. PS I would have been in trouble if you'd cancelled the trip! Xxx

Although she would miss her family, knowing they were only a call or a text away made her feel less lonely.

After breakfast and a thorough read of the newspaper, in a small cobblestoned patio area that had an outdoor table setting for two under a pergola covered in grape vines, Phoebe felt even more positive about her temporary stay in Australia. She was actually enjoying this time to herself, and she decided after completing the crossword and finishing her freshly squeezed orange juice that Heath's suggestion of spending some time swimming wouldn't be so bad.

She could do with some sun. A long, relaxing swim at the beach or in a pool was just what the doctor ordered. With no preference, but also no idea where to go, she looked up some local beaches and public pools on the internet.

The beach, she discovered, would mean a thirty-minute tram trip to Glenelg, or there was a pool about a ten-minute cab ride away in Burnside. She opted for the pool.

Searching in her suitcase, she found her floral bikini, sarong and sunblock. She slipped on the bikini, stepped into her denim shorts and popped a white T-shirt over the top. Then, with a good book, a towel, a wide-brimmed hat and a bottle of water in her beach bag, she called for a cab.

Phoebe had found a perfect spot on the lawn area, adjacent to a huge shade cloth and overlooking the pool. She surmised the sun would get intense later, and she would shift into the shade, but she wanted to enjoy a few minutes of the warm rays and assist her vitamin D intake.

The pool was picturesque, with huge gum trees and parklands surrounding the fenced area. There were quite a few families and some small groups of young mothers with babies enjoying the peaceful ambience of the late morning. Children were laughing and splashing in the crystal water of the wading pool and more serious swimmers were head down, doing lengths of the main pool.

Phoebe had spread out her large blue towel and set up camp. She had spied the fruit in the refrigerator before she'd left home, so she had packed an apple and some strawberries in with her water. Slipping out of her shorts and T-shirt, and putting her hair up atop her head, she strode across the lawn and climbed into the water for a long, relaxing swim.

She was right—it was just what the doctor had ordered. Quite literally.

She lay on her back, lapping the pool slowly and looking up at the stunning blue sky through the filter of her sunglasses. Her worries seemed to dissipate—not completely, but more than she had imagined they would when she had alighted from the plane just a day earlier.

Fifteen minutes later she climbed from the pool and dried herself off with her sun-warmed towel before she spread it out and sat down. With her sarong beside her, in case she needed to cover up, she put on her floppy straw hat, pulled out her book and flipped the lid on her sunblock. She thought of how if she was back in Washington she would be trying to get the ice off her windscreen—instead she was about to cover herself in sunscreen. Perhaps there was justice in the world—or at least a little compensation in the form of sunshine.

She poured a little lotion into her palm and began to rub it over her shoulders.

'Phoebe?'

Phoebe spun around to see Heath standing so tall he was blocking the sun. His chest was bare and his low-slung black swimming trunks left little to her imagination. Beside him was the cutest little boy, with the same blond tousled hair, dinosaur-patterned swim trunks, and a very cheeky smile. But very different eyes. While Heath's were the most vivid blue, his son's huge, twinkling eyes were a stunning deep brown.

'Hello, Heath,' she managed, a little shocked to find him in front of her, and a little more shocked by how gorgeous he looked in even less clothing than the day before.

'I didn't expect to see you here. I didn't think you'd actually take my advice about getting some sun and a swim.'

'It sounded like a good idea,' she replied, trying not to show how embarrassed she felt in choosing the same outdoor pool as Heath. He had described the city as a large country town, but now she wondered how small Adelaide was to have found them in the same place. 'And I do need to get some vitamin D.'

As she said it Phoebe realised she was wearing only a string bikini, and suddenly felt very self-conscious. She hadn't thought twice about it with the other pool guests, as she didn't know them, but for some reason she felt more exposed in front of Heath. She wanted to reach for her sarong and bring it up to her neck, but realised how silly she would appear.

Heath sensed that Phoebe was feeling awkward in that very brief and very stunning bikini. He had witnessed her discomfiture the previous day, when she had been so intent on tugging her skirt into place. But suddenly his eyes just naturally began to roam her body. Every curve was perfect, he thought, before he quickly slipped on his sunglasses, then turned his attention back to his son. Where it had to stay.

'Oscar.' Heath began ruffling the little boy's hair with his hand. 'This is Phoebe—she'll be working with me for the next month, while Grandpa gets better.'

'Hello, Phoebe,' the little boy responded. 'You're pretty—like Aunty Tilly.'

Phoebe felt herself blush. 'Thank you, Oscar, that is a very nice thing to say.'

'It's the truth,' he replied. 'My kindy teacher isn't as pretty as you, but she can sing really well. Can you sing?'

'No, I'm afraid I can't.'

'That's okay. Don't feel bad. My grandpa can't sing either—he tries in the shower, but it sounds terrible and the dog next door barks. He barks a *lot*. I don't know if Daddy can sing. I've never heard him try to sing. Even when there's Christmas carols he never sings along.'

'That's because my voice is worse than Grandpa's,' Heath added, knowing his inability to sing Christmas carols had nothing to do with the quality of his voice. There was much more to it than that. 'It's best I don't try or the dog next door might run away.'

'You're silly, Daddy. The dog can't open the gate.'

Phoebe smiled at their happy banter. It was the first time she had seen a full smile from Heath. The other time there had been only the hint of a smile. She thought he should do it more often.

'Can I go in the pool now? Can I? Can I? Please, Daddy?' Oscar's words became faster and louder as they came rushing out.

'Sure can.' Heath said, eager to move away from Phoebe in her skimpy bathing suit. 'I hope you enjoy your time here today, Phoebe,' he added before he took his son's hand. 'If you need anything we're not too far away.'

'Thanks, I'm sure I will be just fine.'

Heath positioned his sunglasses on the top of his head, nodded in Phoebe's direction and then reached for his son's hand and walked towards the water's edge.

Phoebe suddenly felt a little shiver run all over her body. She ignored it. She had no intention of asking Heath for anything or paying any attention to her body's inappropriate reaction to her boss. It was her hormones, simply out of sorts after the emotional rollercoaster of the last few months, she decided. Perhaps jet-lag was playing a part too.

She had worked with some very attractive medics over the years and he was just another one—nothing more, she thought as she reached for her book. Once Heath Rollins exited from the practice she would never see him again. And that was how she wanted her life to remain. No men and all about her career.

Heath loved being with his son. He always gave him one hundred per cent of his attention when they were together. Oscar was his reason for getting up every day, although he never let the little boy feel that pressure or carry that load. He didn't want his family to attempt to change that dynamic or to question his reasons for still being alone five years after Natasha's death. His choices were no one else's business. He would cover for his father at the practice and then return to Sydney, where he and Oscar would live life the way he wanted. With no interference or futile attempts at matchmaking.

Heath knew that no woman would ever replace Natasha. And, even more than that, he thought every day of how Natasha had been denied the joy of watching her child grow into a man. Some days were harder than others. The sadness, the guilt, the emptiness... Aside from Oscar, Heath's work was his saviour. It was a distraction that gave him purpose.

But today he felt as if someone else was pulling his thoughts away momentarily. Someone who was not only academically and professionally astute, and beautiful from head to toe, but whose humility appeared genuine. But, he reminded himself as he took Oscar to the bigger pool for a father-son swimming lesson, he barely knew her and he was happy with his life just the way it was. He had Oscar and he had his career and that had been enough for him for five years.

He slipped small brightly coloured goggles over his son's eyes and held him securely, encouraging him to take big strokes and put his head under the water, and he didn't look back in Phoebe's direction. Not once.

Despite her best efforts, Phoebe couldn't concentrate on her book. Initially she thought it was tiredness that made her read and reread the same sentence until there was no point continuing. But then she realised it was curiosity, or something like it, that drew her to glance back at Heath and his son. Through her sunglasses Phoebe could see how the two were incredibly close, and the love between them was palpable. Heath looked to be the perfect father, and watching them made Phoebe smile just a little.

She had never thought too much about having children. She'd assumed she would, and had looked forward to being a mother one day, but it hadn't been a driving force in her life. Unlike some of her friends, who had set a date by which they wanted to have the picket fence and three children, Phoebe liked to live her life as it unfolded and had never been one to over-plan. She had spent so long studying, achieving her career goals through long hours at the hospital and in surgery, and then she had got caught up in the wedding…

She blinked away memories that needed to be forgotten and decided, sitting on her damp towel in the sticky heat and looking up at the towering gum trees, that this would be the day she packed them away for good. The pain, the disappointment and the humiliation had no place in her life. She didn't know what did have a place exactly, but the sadness seemed to be fading in the warmth of the Australian sun and Phoebe finally felt good about life. Three months in the same cold town hadn't helped, but the distance and the glorious summer weather appeared to be working. Her decision to set sail was one she felt a little surer she would not regret.

With her mind wandering, she hadn't noticed the two handsome men walking towards her. Both dripping wet, they stood at the bottom of her towel and she came back to the present with a jolt. But a very pleasant one.

'I hope we didn't scare you. You looked like you were a million miles away.'

'About ten thousand, to be exact.'

'You're homesick for Washington already?' Heath asked, almost hoping she would confirm his thoughts and tell him she was planning on returning immediately to the US. That would be fortuitous news for him, because he had a gut feeling that Phoebe's presence might bring complications into his otherwise contained life.

'Not at all,' she replied honestly and, being completely clueless to his hopes, she had lightness in her voice. 'I was just thinking about how lucky I am to be melting rather than freezing.'

'If you were a chocolate bar you wouldn't say that!' Oscar told her with a big smile, before he scampered back to the wading pool and signalled to his father to follow.

Phoebe watched Oscar run in and out of the pool for the best part of an hour, and she found it difficult not to occasionally look at Heath, who stood watch over his son. She walked to the far end of the pool, as she didn't want to infringe on Heath and Oscar's time together. He was a single father, who no doubt worked long hours like most medical professionals, so their time together as father and son was precious. She was surprised that a man who said

he didn't like to compromise certainly appeared to let his
son make the rules.

Sitting on the pool edge, she dangled her legs into the
water and thought for the first time in her life she had no
future plans. Past these next six months in Adelaide she
had no clue where she would go. Perhaps back to Washington—perhaps not. There was a newfound security in
having no security in place. Nothing set in stone. And
no one to let her down since she only had herself to rely
upon. No man to break her heart and shatter her dreams.
She had a temporary job and an income and that was all
she really needed for the time being.

Phoebe Johnson was finally sailing her own ship and
she liked it. She hoped that in this town, so far from everyone she knew, she might possibly find herself. But not for a
very long time did she want to share her heart, her bed or
potentially her future with a man—if indeed she ever did.

She pulled her legs out of the water and headed back
to her towel, where she ate her apple and her strawberries
and then felt her stomach rumble. It was time to go back
to her house for lunch, she decided, and began to pack up
her belongings. Heath and Oscar were lying in the shade,
eating ice cream, so she waved and quietly headed out to
the main road. She planned on hailing a passing cab.

After five minutes, with no sign of any passing cabs,
she reached into her bag to dial for one.

'Daddy, look—there's Phoebe. Is she waiting for her daddy
to pick her up?'

'I don't think so, Oscar. She just arrived in town and
her father lives in another country a long way from here.'

'Then we need to take her home. That would be a nice
thing to do.'

Although part of him knew extending an invitation to

share a ride home was close to the last thing he should do, given his desire to stay away from Phoebe when she had so little clothing on, Heath knew it was the right thing to do. Phoebe knew no one, and she was stranded at the pool after she'd taken him up on his suggestion. She had at least now put shorts on.

There was only one thing to do, he knew, as he took Oscar's hand and walked slowly over to Phoebe.

'Can we offer you a ride home?'

Phoebe had accepted the ride back to her home with a still mostly serious Heath and his very excited and happy little boy. She assumed Oscar had inherited his outgoing personality from his mother. The conversation came predominantly from the back seat, where Oscar was recalling his swimming prowess, until they drew near to her house.

'I'm here on the left—well, I think I am,' she said, then paused as she questioned the accuracy of her directions. 'I tried to notice the way the cab driver took me and reverse it in my head.'

'It's two down on the right, actually. I have your address,' he told her as he ignored her directions and kept driving. 'I noted it from your personal records, which were transferred with the immigration form. It's listed as your residence for the next six months.'

Phoebe could sense he was being a little condescending, and while he wasn't exactly rude she still didn't take kindly to it. She had only been in the country two days, and she thought even to be in the close vicinity of her new home was quite good. She doubted *he'd* do any better if the tables were turned and he was dropped into Washington.

'Well, maybe it was transcribed incorrectly and maybe it was the street you just passed—on the *left*.'

Heath sensed she was being petulant and he found it

almost amusing. He had grown up in Adelaide and knew the street she was referring to was home to a food market and some restaurants—not houses.

'Fine, then I'm happy to turn around and drop you back in the street you think is yours.'

Phoebe knew he had called her bluff, and on such a hot day he had won.

'No, let's do it your way and see if you're right.'

'Let's.'

'You sound like Aunty Tilly and Uncle Paul,' Oscar suddenly announced from the back seat. 'They talk like that all the time, but in the end Aunty Tilly always wins.'

Heath froze, and so did Phoebe. Heath knew he was talking about his sister and brother-in-law—a married couple—and that Phoebe would suspect as much. They both went silent, and the rest of the short trip was dedicated to Oscar's chatter about the pool.

It wasn't long before Phoebe found herself waving good-bye and thanking her travelling companions before making her way inside her house. Oscar's comment still resonated with her long after she'd closed the front door. *They'd sounded like a married couple bickering.*

Initially, looking over at her handsome, almost brooding chauffeur, with his wet hair slicked back and his shirt buttoned low over his lightly tanned chest, she'd felt herself wondering what might have been had they met under different circumstances…before she had been hurt so terribly by Giles.

But as she tried to forget that heartbreak she couldn't deny that her heart beat a little faster being so close to Heath. His nearness had made her play self-consciously with loose wisps of her hair and swallow nervously more than once as she had looked away from his direction and to the scenery outside of the car during the trip home.

But she wasn't interested in men and particularly not pompous men who took enjoyment in proving they were right. And romance only brought anguish into her life, she reminded herself. After Oscar's bombshell she'd realised she had to step back. Right away from any contact with Heath outside of work arrangements, she decided as she dropped her bag of wet things into the laundry.

Pushing the child's observation out of her mind, Phoebe made some lunch. What could Oscar really know about married couples? Nothing, she told herself, and decided to call her father. It was late in Washington, but he had left a message on her phone so she knew he was still awake.

'So, what do you think of Adelaide?'

Phoebe wasn't sure what to tell her father. She hadn't seen much of the city, save for the airport, a coffee shop, a stifling hot podiatric practice and of course the pool, so her experience was limited. Her view of the parklands was lovely, but she had kept inside a small radius since arriving so thought she wasn't yet placed to give a great evaluation. And when it came to the people of Adelaide she had spoken to the customs official, her cab drivers, Heath, Oscar and momentarily Tilly.

Not really enough to gauge a whole town, she thought. Immigration had been pleasant, the cab drivers were polite, Tilly seemed sweet, Oscar was cute—and then there was Heath. She really didn't want to spend time thinking about him. Particularly after Oscar's comment.

She was confused, but pushed thoughts of him to the back of her mind. He was a conundrum that she wasn't sure she cared to solve. It could be another woman's problem, she decided. One good-looking man had already taken too much of her time and energy with no reward. And she was definitely not looking for a replacement. No matter how handsome.

'It's super-hot,' she finally replied.

'That's it?' Her father laughed heartily. 'You fly to the other side of the world and all you can tell me about the city is that it's super-hot? Wouldn't want *you* to be the only witness for the prosecution any time soon.'

Phoebe realised how vague it had sounded, and she also knew she didn't need to have her guard up. Her father knew the worst that had happened.

'I met Dr Rollins, and the practice is great, but the air-conditioning has broken down so we just had coffee yesterday, and today I went for a swim since I have the day off while it gets repaired.'

'So Ken Rollins is a good man? Do you think you'll enjoy working with him?'

Phoebe drew breath. She wished she could answer in the affirmative to both questions but she couldn't. She hadn't met Ken.

'Ken's undergone emergency knee surgery, so his son is looking after the practice.'

'It's fortunate for him that he has a son to take over,' her father replied, then added thoughtfully, 'But I know you were looking forward to working with Ken after you read his papers. I hope you're not disappointed?'

It was the second time she had been asked that question. And her answer still stood. She wasn't disappointed. Confused about the man, and definitely not interested beyond their working relationship, but not disappointed.

'Working with Heath will be a learning experience.'

'I hope you enjoy it, then,' he told his daughter.

'I hope so too, and if nothing else I've got a few months of warm weather ahead,' she said, trying to remind herself of the only benefit she should be considering.

'Try feeling sorry for your father. I'll be shovelling snow at some ungodly hour in the morning. Perhaps you should get some sleep, sweetie. Your flight would have been taxing, and the high temperatures will add to that.'

'It was a little tiring, but I think...' Phoebe paused as she heard the beeping of a text message come through. 'Can you hold for one minute, Dad? I think I got a message...'

'Sure, honey.'

Phoebe pulled the phone away from her ear and saw a number she didn't know. She recognised it as local and read the message.

Phoebe, it's Tilly. I know it's late notice, but would you be free for dinner tonight around seven at my place? Dad will be here and he'd love to meet you. And I would love to chat properly. Heath can pick you up.

An invitation to have dinner with the family was something Phoebe hadn't expected and she felt her errant heart race a little with the prospect of seeing Heath again. She knew it was crazy but her response to seeing him again made it obvious she may have a battle ahead. It clearly wasn't going to be as easy as telling herself the facts. She couldn't look out of a car window and ignore her reaction. She had to look inside of herself and face the fact that Heath was awakening feelings that she thought she had packed away when she had decided to focus on her career. Suddenly butterflies began to quicken in her stomach.

She didn't answer the text immediately as she quickly made plans in her head. She couldn't decline as that would be rude. And she wanted to meet Ken. With her breathing still a little strained, she resolved to get a taxi there on the pretext of saving Heath the trip—when she was only too aware it was to avoid the closeness of him in the confines of his car.

'I'm back,' she said, trying to concentrate once again on the conversation with her father. 'How's Mother?'

'She's fine. At her yoga class and then off to have a manicure, I think—or maybe it's to have her hair done. I can't remember. My day's been taken up with a new healthcare bill that the President wants to pass through Congress. It's a struggle, but you know me, I'm always up for a challenge.'

'Always—and you're so good at it.'

'Thanks, but the apple didn't fall too far from the tree. Look at you. Going to the other side of the world after what you've been through is quite the challenge too.'

'Hardly going to change the world here—and you did all the work. I really do appreciate you arranging everything. The house is wonderful, and it's stocked for a hungry army. Thank you so much.'

'You are more than welcome—but, speaking of an army, I'd better go, honey,' her father cut in. 'Urgent briefing with the Secretary of Defence at six a.m. tomorrow, so I'd better get some sleep before I head out in the wee hours of the morning with salt and a shovel to clear the driveway.'

'Okay, Dad. Love you.'

'Back at you—and I hope you have fun, whatever you do.'

Phoebe went into her room and collapsed into the softness of her bed, dropping the mobile phone beside her. She decided to take a shower and think logically about the invitation before rushing in. Perhaps she should decline and meet Ken another time. Perhaps she should avoid Heath in a social situation. Keep it purely professional the way it should be. Stepping under tepid water, Phoebe washed her hair, and by the time she had rinsed out the conditioner she had come to the conclusion that she had to stop overthinking the situation.

Oscar's remark had thrown her, and Heath's attitude had been a little patronizing, but he was right—he had known the way to her home. And she hadn't. Perhaps she had been a little defensive for no reason other than to push him away.

Her head was spinning and it wasn't the heat. Her house was wonderfully cool.

'Get a grip, Phoebe Johnson. Stop creating false drama where there is none. Heath Rollins is not interested in you. It's dinner with Ken's family and that's it. Almost business. And Oscar was way off the mark. He's only a child, and no judge of what married couples *really* sound like. You have nothing to worry about. Heath Rollins is not looking for love any more than you.'

So she accepted the invitation…with the proviso that she would catch a cab.

# CHAPTER FIVE

'PHOEBE SEEMS LOVELY,' Tilly said as she placed a large bowl of homemade potato salad on the dining table, where Heath, Oscar, Ken, her husband Paul and her two daughters were seated, waiting for Phoebe to arrive.

Heath watched as Paul, a tall man with an athletic build, by trade an engineer who directed huge construction teams, struggled to keep his tiny girls from climbing down from their booster chairs and heading back to their toys. He was clearly losing the battle, and one of them took off across the room, so he surrendered and set the girls up with a picnic blanket on the floor, added some toys and invited Oscar to join them.

Tilly was a wonderful cook, who never liked to see anyone leave hungry, so she had grilled a selection of chicken shashlik, vegetable patties and gourmet sausages from her local butcher, along with her famous potato salad and a Greek salad.

'Can someone please remind me why she's coming to dinner? She's here to work—not join family gatherings, surely?'

'It's called being hospitable to a stranger in town, Heath. And she's lovely, as I said.'

'Yes, she's nice.' Oscar seconded his aunt's opinion of

Phoebe as he stood up and strained to reach for a slice of bread from the table.

Smiling, his grandfather slid the plate closer to him to make the task easier.

'You met her too, Oscar?' Tilly asked as she brought cold drinks to the table.

'Yes, at the pool,' Oscar responded as he sat down with his twin cousins again, a big slice of bread in his hand. 'And we drove her home and she and Daddy talked a lot.'

'So you all went to the pool together, then?' Tilly addressed her question to Heath, her eyes smiling.

'I took Oscar to the Burnside pool and Phoebe happened to be there,' he responded defensively.

He had experienced more than a few attempts by his sister to matchmake over the years, and he intended to quash this attempt immediately. He wasn't buying into her supposedly casual conversation that would no doubt lead to something more like an interrogation over his love-life if he allowed it.

'So, of all the pools in Adelaide, a woman who knows nothing of Adelaide just happened to choose that one?'

Heath's silence was his answer.

'So everyone has met the doctor I hired except me?' Ken asked. 'Well, at least I'll get to meet her tonight and judge for myself.'

'*I* haven't met her yet,' Paul said. 'But then I didn't know you'd even hired anyone—I thought Heath was filling in for you.'

'He is. But the practice is growing, and I needed help, and Dr Phoebe Johnson was highly recommended. I had made arrangements for her to work with me before the accident. From all accounts she's a brilliant young podiatric surgeon looking for a change of scenery, so I jumped at the chance. Pardon the pun,' he said as he looked down at his bandaged knee.

'Very pretty too,' Tilly remarked.

'I hadn't heard that part, but it never hurts to have a pretty doctor in the practice,' said the older Dr Rollins. 'So, Heath, do you think you two will get along?'

Heath considered the question and answered in his usual guarded tones. 'I've read her transcripts and she has an impressive record—and the reports from the Washington hospital are great. We chatted yesterday morning at the café for a while, and she seems suited to the role.'

'Yesterday morning? You mean you took her out after she fainted? Quick work, Heath. I'm impressed,' said Tilly.

'Phoebe fainted? Is she okay?' Ken asked.

'I didn't *take her out*—we had a cool drink to talk about work and, yes, Dad, Phoebe's fine. The heat just got to her but I'm sure we won't have a repeat once the air-con is up and running again. You might like to consider renovating the building in the not too distant future.'

He'd added that to change an obvious subject direction that he didn't like.

'I could do you a rebuild,' Paul chipped in. 'Bulldoze and start again. Prime real estate there, and I've been saying for years the old building has had its day.'

Ken looked stony-faced at his son-in-law, to end that line of conversation, and then turned back to Heath. 'So, when my newest employee is conscious and upright, *is* she pretty?'

Heath looked around the table and realised they were all poised for his reply. 'Yes, she's pretty.'

Tilly smiled a self-satisfied smile, while Ken nodded to himself and Paul winked at his wife.

Heath saw the looks they gave each other and lowered his voice so that Oscar wouldn't hear the adults' conversation. 'Just because I made mention of Phoebe's appearance, don't think for a minute that I'm interested in her. It was a response to a direct question. Don't try and set us up. I don't need anyone in my life, and if you try anything you'll be short one staff member. *Me.* I'll be on a plane back to Sydney faster than you can blink. Neither Oscar or I need anyone else in our lives.'

'Are you sure about that?' Tilly asked with a brazen look.

'Yes. You know how I feel. It's been just Oscar and me for the last five years. No woman has come into our lives.'

'I know, but now Phoebe has. And you've already broken one of your unbreakable rules with her. *No woman shall meet your son.* Well, she has and he seems to like her.'

Just then the doorbell rang, and Heath stood up and walked briskly past the Christmas tree that Tilly had decorated that morning. It was the second time he had walked past it that evening, and both times he had looked at it only briefly and then looked away without making mention of it. He was still not able to face Christmas and all the trimmings. He doubted he ever would again. There was nothing that could make him enjoy the holiday season. He had tried and failed. Christmas was just too painful.

As he opened the door Oscar ran over to join him.

'Hello, Phoebe!' Oscar called out excitedly before Heath had a chance to greet her. 'Aunty Tilly has cooked lots of food, so I hope you're hungry.'

'Hello, Oscar,' she replied, and smiled at his toothy grin and cheeky smile before he ran off, allowing her to lift her gaze to greet Heath. 'Hello.'

Heath drew a deep breath. Phoebe looked gorgeous. She wore a deep blue halter dress. Her skin was pale against the fabric and looked like delicate porcelain, and her hair was falling in soft curls around her shoulders. Her beauty was not lost on him.

'Hi, Phoebe—come in.'

He moved back from the doorway and as she stepped inside he couldn't help but notice as she brushed past him that the back of her dress was cut low and revealed even more of her bare skin. His pulse instantly, and against his will, picked up speed.

'Phoebe,' Tilly said as she opened her arms to greet her dinner guest. 'So lovely you could make it. It's only casual, but I thought you could meet Dad and chat over a bite to eat since he was feeling a little left out.'

'It's my pleasure—thank you so much for inviting me,' she said, and then, spying the huge Christmas tree, she couldn't help but comment. 'That is a *gorgeous* tree, Tilly. Christmas truly is my favourite time of year.'

The two women walked into the dining room and on their way Phoebe gave her hostess some chocolates she had brought as a thank-you gift. Heath followed, and after hearing the Christmas comment realised that he and Phoebe had less in common than he'd first thought. She was a professional woman, and he had hoped she wouldn't be the nostalgic type. Apparently, he'd been wrong.

He couldn't deny to himself that Phoebe was stunning, and in that dress desirable, but he wasn't looking for a woman to share his life the way his family thought he should. And one night with Phoebe in his bed wouldn't work any way he looked at it. It would only complicate his life on so many levels, and that was something he didn't need.

As they entered the dining room, Ken was chatting with Paul.

'The simple joy of enjoying a pale ale any time I like is my compensation for not being able to operate. But believe me, I would prefer to have the use of my gammy knee than to be sitting around all day,' Ken said, then paused as he caught sight of Phoebe. 'Please excuse my bad manners and not standing to meet you,' he continued with an outstretched hand. 'I'm Ken Rollins, and you must be Dr Phoebe Johnson.'

Phoebe stepped closer to Ken and met his handshake. 'Yes, I'm Phoebe, and I'm very happy to finally meet you.'

Ken was impressed with the grip in her handshake. 'For a slender woman you have a strong handshake. But then you're a surgeon, so a strong and steady grip is a prerequisite for our shared field of medicine.'

Phoebe wasn't sure how to react, so she smiled.

'Please—sit down, I didn't mean to embarrass you. And sit next to *me*. I want to hear everything about you that wasn't written down on your incredibly impressive résumé. I'm sure there's lots to know.'

'Fire away,' she managed to return as she took her seat at the table, hoping his questions would be broad enough to avoid the awkward moments in her recent history.

Tilly began handing the platters of food around and soon everyone was filling their plates, while Paul put the children's food on their picnic blanket for them to share, then returned to join the adults.

'So why Adelaide?' Ken asked as he took a serving of Greek salad, ensuring there was plenty of feta cheese and olives on his plate.

'The chance to work with you,' Phoebe replied. 'I read your most recent paper on improvements to prescribed orthotic devices to control motion and position of the leg during locomotion and I think your work is outstanding. The chance to have you mentor me was too good to pass up.'

'Well, I must say that is lovely to hear, and I look

forward to working with you once my knee is tickety-
boo again,' he told her, with a hint of pride in his expression. 'So tell me about your family. I picked up from
our correspondence that your father works at the White
House.'

Ken reached for another shashlik and held the plate so
that Phoebe could take one as well.

'Yes, he's an advisor to the President. He's been in the
world of politics for over nineteen years. He was in international banking before that.'

'And you weren't tempted to follow him into the political arena?' Heath cut in.

'Not at all. You see, you're right—it's an arena, and
that's why I wouldn't do it. Sometimes it's great, but at
other times it seems like a fight to the death. I'd rather be
repairing bodies than ripping apart political opponents
and their policies.'

'Touché,' Ken replied with a huge smile.

'Still, it must be an interesting lifestyle,' Tilly commented. 'Do you visit the White House often?'

'Now and then. But my place is the other side of town,
nearer to the hospital. I just hear about it when I visit or
call my parents.'

'I suppose it would be a little like the emergency department of a hospital—with everyone rushing frantically
and everything code blue,' Tilly replied.

Phoebe smiled at her. 'You're not too far wrong with
that analogy. It's like everything needs to be delivered or
decided yesterday. I would most certainly go mad. My father, however, loves a challenge—he sees the big picture
and the changes that need to be made for the disadvan-
taged and most particularly those with intergenerational
problems.'

'And your mother? What does she do?' Ken asked between bites.

'Anything and everything social. Fundraising committees, women's political auxiliaries—pretty much anything that she believes helps with my father's career. Along with her bridge club.'

'So why did you choose medicine?' Ken asked. 'With a father in politics and, for want of a better word, a socialite mother, why did you choose to specialise in podiatric surgery?'

'My best friend Susy's mother had an accident driving us to school when I was fourteen...' Phoebe began.

Feeling a little parched from answering all the questions, took a sip of her cold drink before she continued.

'Anyway, she broke her heel and I was there when the paramedics took her by ambulance to the hospital. Susy and I had both been strapped in the back of the car and didn't suffer even a scratch. I visited her mother in hospital a few times with Susy, and I became curious and started asking the nurses questions. Then one day her podiatric surgeon came in. I asked him all about the operation and he went into great detail with me and that was it. I knew what I wanted to do with my life.'

'I'm impressed that you knew at such a young age—'

'I think that we should let poor Phoebe eat,' Tilly cut in. 'She's been grilled and she's passed with flying colours, Dad, so now she gets fed and watered.'

They all smiled, and then chatted about themselves so Phoebe could enjoy the delicious dinner Tilly had prepared and also get to know the family.

Everyone but Heath told her something about themselves and their lives. Heath stayed quiet, and Phoebe noticed his jaw clench more than a few times as they talked about Oscar as a baby. It was obvious to Phoebe that it had been a difficult time for him. But why exactly she wasn't sure, and they all clearly avoided the topic of Oscar's mother.

'Do you want to look at the stars?' Oscar suddenly asked Phoebe as she sat waiting for Heath to bring a drink out to the patio, where everyone had moved after dinner to enjoy the balmy evening.

'Do you have a telescope?'

'No, but we can lie on the grass and look up and see them. That's one of my favourite things to do at night. Grandpa knows lots about stars.'

Phoebe thought it was a lovely idea, and very sweet of Oscar to extend the invitation for her to join him. She stepped out of her shoes and followed him to a patch of lawn just near the patio, where they both lay down on the grass and looked up at the stars twinkling in the ebony sky. The cool ground beneath her bare skin felt wonderful.

'That's the saucepan. Can you see it? You have to draw a line between the big star—up there—and the others—just there—and it looks like a saucepan,' he said, pointing his tiny finger straight up in the air. 'And it has a handle too.'

'I can see it,' she responded as she looked to where he pointed.

They both lay staring at the perfect night sky and Oscar talked with lightning speed about everything his grandfather had told him. Phoebe was impressed with all he had retained, and his interest in astronomy.

'Perhaps you might grow up and study the stars,' she said. 'That would make you an astronomer.'

'I think I might visit them instead.'

'So you want to be an astronaut?'

'Yes. That would be more fun than just looking at them.'

Heath stood in the doorway to the patio and looked out

at the two of them, lying in the dark on the lawn, talking. He had no idea what they were saying but he could hear their animated chatter. He felt a tug at his heart, thinking that his wife had missed out on doing just that. And that Oscar had missed out on those important long talks with his mother.

They had both been cheated. And even though his pain lessened with every passing year he wondered if Oscar's would grow as he realised what he had lost.

"You know, Phoebe's nothing like I imagined,' Ken said softly when he saw Heath in the doorway with Phoebe's drink.

Heath agreed with his father's sentiments but he would not let him know. He wouldn't let any family member know, for fear of them trying to make a spark ignite between them. He had found her to be sweet when they'd first met, sexy at the pool, and looking at her now, lying beside his son, he was discovering she was apparently maternal—but that wasn't a combination he wanted. He preferred sexy with no strings attached, for one-night stands that could never break his heart. Or impact on his son.

'I think we should probably get going,' he said to his father. 'I need to get Oscar to bed—and you as well, Dad.'

'Don't fuss about getting me to bed, son,' Ken told him as he watched Oscar and Phoebe. 'I'm quite enjoying the company and I'm not that old yet. But, having said that, I imagine young Oscar might be getting tired after a day out.'

'Let him spend the night with us,' Tilly offered as she stepped outside and was pleasantly surprised to see her nephew relaxing on the lawn with Phoebe. 'Then we can get up early and have a swim before it gets hot. I think he's a little lonely over at Dad's. I can do some things with him that you—'

'That I can't do because they are things only a mother can do?'

'No, Heath. Not even close,' Tilly replied in a gentle tone. 'You're doing an amazing job with Oscar. He's adorable and polite and I love him to bits—you know that. But it's hard with you working long hours, and Dad can't do anything while he's laid up, so I thought I'd help out and do something fun while you're stepping in for Dad. Stop being so hard on yourself.'

'I'm not being hard—I'm a realist, and I think Oscar is out of his routine over here. He probably misses his nanny and preschool. Once he gets back to Sydney he'll be fine again.'

'I'm sure you're right. But in the meantime let me have him for a day.'

'Tilly's enjoying having you both in Adelaide,' Paul added. 'And I'm sure she wants to make the most of it. It doesn't happen often enough.'

'Absolutely,' Tilly agreed. 'Check with Oscar and see if he's up for it...'

'Up for what?' Oscar and Phoebe had left their observation spot on the lawn and walked up quietly without the others noticing.

'A sleepover and a day with us tomorrow.'

'Sure am—then I can go swimming with Aunty Tilly in the morning. Can I, Daddy, *please*?'

'Well, I guess the decision has been made,' Heath said, not having expected Oscar to jump at the idea of a sleepover so quickly. He'd thought they were joined at the hip, but perhaps that tie was loosening. And maybe he did need to let Tilly mother him now and then.

'Do you want to sleep over too, Phoebe? And Daddy could too?'

Heath's eyes widened in surprise at Oscar's invitation to both of them.

Phoebe smiled. 'That's very kind of you, but I have to go home to my own bed and my pyjamas.'

'I sleep in my T-shirt and jocks in summer,' Oscar cut in, with a serious tone in his little voice. 'You could do the same.'

They all smiled at Oscar's matter-of-fact response—well, everyone bar Heath. He was still thinking about the void in his son's life that was becoming more and more obvious. It was one that he'd thought he had managed to fill.

'Perhaps another time,' Phoebe said politely, thinking that there was no way she would be stripping down to her underwear for a sleepover with Heath.

Tilly tried not to laugh as she hugged her nephew and, looking at his food-stained T-shirt, she directed a request to Heath. 'Could you drop off some fresh clothes tomorrow morning in case we want to go out?'

Still deep in thought, he responded, 'Sure—as long as you're sure it's not too much trouble for him to stay?'

'Not at all,' Tilly said as she picked up Oscar and put him on her lap. 'Early-morning swim for you and me, Oscar—and, Phoebe, if you're not doing anything please come over and join us for a swim.'

Phoebe was surprised at how warm and welcoming the family was, and was very quickly feeling at home, but she declined, thinking that perhaps the offer was Tilly just being courteous.

Heath looked at his sister and then back at Phoebe without saying a word, then he kissed his son goodnight and walked out to the car. He was glad Phoebe had not accepted. She was becoming too close to his family too quickly. And starting to get under his skin a little too. He understood why she was a perfect fit for his family, with her down-to-earth personality, quick wit and sense of fun. He was also very aware that those same traits combined with her beauty were making her far too desirable to him. And he didn't like it.

She could leave at any minute, and that wouldn't be fair to Oscar. He didn't want him to grow close to a person who would walk away. He needed to protect his son from that pain. And, more than that, he didn't want their life to change.

'I will see you in the morning,' he called out before he drove away, with his father and Phoebe in the car.

The sun was setting as the three of them drove through the city to Phoebe's home. Each one was thinking about the same thing. How quickly and naturally Phoebe was seeming to fit into their lives. Ken was thrilled; Phoebe was surprised—Heath was more worried than he had been in a very long time...

# CHAPTER SIX

HEATH WOKE AT four and lay staring out his window to the
dark sky that was softly lit by a haze-covered moon. He
knew the warm air outside would be heavy and still. He
rolled onto his back and lifted his arms above his head and
thought back over the previous two days, since Phoebe had
fallen into his arms.

He didn't want to be thinking about her—and especially not at four in the morning, lying in bed—but her face
wouldn't leave his mind. When Phoebe had been close to
him—close enough for him to smell the scent that rested
delicately on her skin and close enough to see the sparkle
in her beautiful green eyes—he had struggled to remember why he didn't want a woman in his life on any permanent basis.

But that was something he had to remember. Particularly now.

His life had begun to change since he'd arrived back
in Adelaide.

He had worried for a little while that the life he had built
with his son, just the two of them, might not be enough
for Oscar one day. And he feared now that that day was
almost upon him. But he didn't want to lose control. Once
before he had lost control of a situation—lost his wife and

almost lost his mind. He wouldn't let it happen again. He needed to remain in control and not blindly accept change.

And he couldn't accept Phoebe as the catalyst for that change.

He was more than concerned after seeing how comfortable the family had been with her. It was moving too fast for him. He had to put the brakes on the level of intimacy he thought they were all building with her. It needed to stop immediately. The air-conditioning repairman had notified him that the work was completed at the practice and while there were no patients booked in until the next day, he would send Phoebe a message just after nine and ask her to call into the practice to go over the patient notes. That would serve his purpose.

He needed to remind her why she was there—and it wasn't to grow close to any member of his family, and particularly not his son. It was a relationship he didn't want to see develop and risk it being torn apart when they headed back to Sydney and Phoebe headed back to her home country.

Phoebe woke early, picked up the paper and was halfway through the crossword when she got the call just after eight.

'Hi, Phoebe—it's Tilly. Would you like to jump in a cab and have breakfast by the pool with us? I'd pick you up, but by the time I load the diaper gang you could already be here.'

'I'm not sure…' She hesitated to accept the invitation. 'This is your time with Oscar. I don't want to infringe on that.'

'Nonsense. I would love to chat to another adult. Away from the surgery my days are filled with nursery rhymes and potty-training, and Oscar could do with another set of eyes on him while he's in the pool. It is hard with three of them, and my stomach is in a knot trying to keep a watch over them all. At their age it's a bit like herding cats.'

'Well, if you're sure I can help, I'd love to.'

'It's settled, then,' Tilly said. "See you soon—and don't forget your swimsuit.'

Half an hour later Phoebe was alighting from a cab at Tilly's home and a very happy little boy was opening the front door before she'd even reached the doorbell. He was wearing his swimsuit, dry flippers and goggles on the top of his head.

'Hi, Phoebe! Have you got your bathers?'

'Bathers?' she asked as she walked up the paved entrance towards him.

'He means swimsuit,' Tilly said as she invited Phoebe inside. 'In Australia we call a swimsuit bathers. You'll get used to our funny expressions soon enough.'

Phoebe smiled at her hostess, then turned her attention to Oscar, 'Yes, I have my bathers—so I hope you're wanting to swim, because in this weather *I* do!'

Phoebe didn't hear the three text messages from Heath because she was splashing in the pool with his son, and Melissa and Jasmine were excitedly screaming from the sidelines behind the child-safe fence, blocking out all other sounds. Oscar's floating armbands were in place but Phoebe didn't let him go for even a second. They'd had a lovely morning, stopping only for some juice and freshly cut fruit, after which Oscar walked Phoebe around the garden, collecting insects in his bug catcher.

'I only keep them for a few hours, then I let them go back to their daddies…and their mummies. I think some of them have mummies too.'

'I'm sure some of them have both, and some just have

a mummy or a daddy,' Phoebe said, then fell silent as he continued walking, collecting and talking.

Oscar suddenly seemed very deep in thought for a five-year-old, and it worried Phoebe a little.

'My mummy died when I was very little.'

Phoebe felt herself stiffen as he delivered this news. 'I'm sorry to hear that, Oscar.' She paused to gain some composure as her heart went out to the little boy. 'I'm sure she's looking over you every day.'

Phoebe had not considered the prospect that Heath might be a widower. She wasn't sure why it hadn't occurred to her, but now she knew it did go part way to explaining why he was such a serious man, who appeared only to lighten up around his son. Losing his wife and the mother of his child would have been a life-altering tragedy.

'I was very little. I couldn't talk or walk and I don't remember her. But I know her name was—'

'Hello, you two.'

Heath's deep voice suddenly called from the back door, interrupting their conversation and making them both turn abruptly.

Phoebe felt her stomach drop. Then it lifted, and then spun as her heart fluttered nervously. She'd thought she had her reactions to Heath under control, but suddenly she discovered she didn't.

But she had to.

Somehow.

'Hello, Daddy!'

'Hi, Heath.'

Heath quickly crossed to them and dropped to his knees. 'I'm sorry, Oscar, but I'm going to have to take Phoebe to work with me.'

'But we're having *fun*, Daddy, and I want her to stay. She showed me how to swim like a bug and...'

'Swim like a bug?' Heath asked, turning to Phoebe with a curious look on his face.

'The butterfly stroke,' Phoebe said as she looked at this man whom she now knew had suffered the tragedy of losing his wife. It did put a different filter on the way she saw him, but she didn't want him to know that. He seemed too stoic to want pity—in fact she suspected pity would drive him into a darker place.

Despite what she now knew she didn't want it to colour her feelings towards him. She wasn't looking for love and he was obviously still grieving. Although she *was* grateful for the insight, as she would understand his motives a little better and make their working relationship easier. She just had to get her emotions under control. And he was dressed again, as he had been the night before, so it made it easier to concentrate.

'How did you know I was here?' she asked, trying to mask how sad she felt for them both. And how equally drawn she was to the father and son.

'Well, you didn't answer your phone, so on the off-chance that my sister had convinced you to visit I called her and she said you were swimming with Oscar. Unfortunately I'll have to cut that short and ask you to head back to the surgery with me.'

'Like this?' She looked down at her swimsuit covered by a sarong. She had chosen not to wear her bikini that day, and had slipped the one-piece swimsuit under her sarong before she'd left her house. 'But if the air-conditioning isn't running maybe this is the right thing to be wearing.' She tried to be lighthearted. Friendly. At ease. Everything she wasn't feeling.

Heath had tried not to look at her body, but he couldn't help but notice how stunning she looked. He definitely

didn't want to be alone with her at the practice in the out-
fit she was barely wearing.

'Perhaps not,' he replied, trying to avert his eyes from
her petite curves. 'I can drop you home to change, if you'd
like.'

A little while later, after a quick stop at her house for a
change of clothes, they sat reading through the patient
notes in the cool surgery. The newly repaired and effi-
ciently running air-conditioner was working perfectly, but
Phoebe had the distinct feeling that this activity wasn't
really essential. They were straightforward records that
could easily have been read through prior to her meeting
with each patient.

She wondered if it wasn't so much her being at the practice that was important but perhaps more her *not* being
at Tilly's house with Oscar. She wasn't sure why but she
said nothing, and continued to concentrate for the next
two hours on the records that Heath was explaining in
great detail.

Occasionally she would glance at the man across from
her. His chiselled jaw, with a light covering of stubble, was
tense. There was no half-smile. She realised there was no
chance of a full smile and she knew why. Despite her resolve to keep it professional, still she felt her heart pick up
speed a little when their eyes met by accident. And at that
time, they both paused for only a moment in silence. She
didn't know how he was feeling or what he was thinking
but there was something Heath was keeping to himself.

And she suspected it was his heart.

Finally she left to go home. It was a short walk, and she
wanted the time to clear her head. She now knew that
Heath was still suffering from the loss of his wife and al-

though she also knew that Oscar had been little when his mother had died she wasn't sure exactly how long ago it had happened. Three years? Four years? Even five?

But there was one other thing she knew. Heath must have loved his wife very much, and if it had been half as much as he clearly loved Oscar then, although her life had been cut short, his wife had been a very lucky woman to have known that deep a love and commitment. It was something that Phoebe knew she had never experienced. And probably never would.

'Why don't you guys move here permanently?' Tilly asked, sitting down and pouring herself a cold soft drink after dropping Oscar back at her father's later that day. Paul had arrived at her home to mind the twins for a little while. 'I adore Oscar, and I'd love Mels and Jazzy to grow up with their big cousin to keep the boys at bay. I think it makes complete sense.'

'My thoughts exactly,' Ken agreed, while admiring the stunning violet and red hues of the setting sun. The lighting provided a canvas for the silhouettes of the towering gum trees that surrounded his home and the scent of eucalyptus floated in the night air.

But Heath didn't notice anything. He could still remember the scent of Phoebe, sitting so close to him at work, could see her beautiful face, and nothing he did was successful at pushing those images from his mind. He could vaguely hear the mutterings of his father and his sister, but none of it registered. His mind was consumed by thoughts of Phoebe and he felt uneasy. Her sweetness. Her sincerity. She had stumbled into his world and into his arms quite literally, and for some inexplicable reason he couldn't shake her from his thoughts. But he wouldn't break another rule. He had to ignore this fleeting infatuation.

Heath came back to the conversation to see two sets of eyes on him, seeking answers. He didn't like the fact that a family inquisition was developing on the back porch because there was another one going on in his mind and one was more than enough to endure. Two would certainly send him crazy.

'The air-con is now working and that's all that matters. Let's leave it at that. Phoebe is a surgeon, in town to meet the terms of her employment contract. And, by the way, Tilly, she can't be your babysitter.'

'My babysitter? That's a little unfair. She knows no one, and she was alone in her house, and I thought she'd enjoy a swim and a chat. And, FYI, Oscar totally commandeered her for the better part of two hours and that was not my plan—it was his.'

'Well, I'm here only until Dad's knee mends. End of story. So I hope Oscar doesn't get comfortable with the current arrangements. It's all only temporary.'

With that Heath stood up and went inside to find his son. Reading him a story was always a highlight of his day, but that night it would also serve as his avenue of respite from the barrage of questions about Phoebe.

And for a short while it might also silence those inside his head.

'I like Phoebe,' Oscar told his father as he went to turn out the light. 'She's neat.'

'As in tidy?'

'Daddy, you're being *silly*. Not tidy. She's fun—and she makes you happy too.'

Heath was taken aback by his son's words. 'What do you mean by that?'

'Well, I saw you smile. You don't smile very much. I always thought you were sad, but now that Phoebe comes over you're happy more. That makes me happy too. It's almost like we're a family—like Aunty Tilly and Uncle Paul.'

Phoebe called London after she'd eaten her takeaway dinner. She wanted to chat with Susy and hoped with the time difference that while it was evening in Adelaide she would catch her young barrister friend before she left in the morning for court in London.

'Phoebs, how are you?'

'I'm great—how are you, Susy? And how's work? Anything interesting that you can talk about?'

'I'll put you on loud speaker—trying to finish my make-up before I rush out the door.'

'If it's not a good time I'll try another day,' Phoebe said as she rested back into the three soft white pillows on her bed.

The ceiling fan was moving the air above her and Phoebe had opened a window on the approaching darkness. She knew she would be in air-conditioning all of the next day and she wanted to sleep with fresh air, even if it *was* a little warm.

'No, I'm good to talk. Nothing to report. There was a guilty verdict in the grand theft case, which I was thrilled about, and today I'm selecting the jury for a new IT case. Possession of data with intent to commit a serious offence. Same old, same old.' Susy laughed. 'I *do* love my job. We've been securing a high percentage of convictions lately, so it makes it all worthwhile. Unfortunately there's never a shortage of bad guys needing to be put away. But let's forget about me—how are you on your adventure Down Under?'

'It's hot—melting hot, to be accurate.'

'Well, I don't feel even a teeny bit sorry for you, if that's what you're hoping for. I spent last night in my Wellingtons, overcoat and scarf, shovelling snow off my car in case I need it in an emergency. I'll take the Underground into London again today. So, my sister from another mother, stop complaining—'cos while you're over there, getting a suntan, I'm warding off frostbite!'

Both women laughed.

Then Susy's voice became momentarily stern. 'Seriously, Phoebs, has the creep left you alone? And your mother—is she finally coming to terms with the fact that Niles won't be a member of the family?'

'It's Giles…'

'I know…but I prefer to disrespect him at every opportunity, and forgetting his name is a start.'

'I promise he's out of the picture completely. Mother is still not convinced, but I've given up on telling her that cheating is a deal-breaker.'

'Absolutely,' Susy agreed, in her prosecuting barrister tone. 'Guilty, charged and dumped. I do wish there was a way to lock him *and* those tarts away. Pity there's no legal avenue to put the lot of them behind bars and throw away the key.'

'In a perfect world there would be, but I'm trying not to think about him any more. Just onwards and upwards. I'm starting work tomorrow with…Heath.' Phoebe stumbled over his name.

'I thought you were working with Ken Rollins? Who's Heath?'

'His son, actually. Ken needed emergency knee reconstruction. His son's a podiatric surgeon too, so he's stepped in to help out for the next few weeks.'

'I hope you're not disappointed? I know you were really excited to be working with Ken.'

This was now the third time she had been asked and still her answer remained the same. Disappointed, no…

confused, yes…and now she was feeling a little melancholy about what had made Heath the man he was.

'I was looking forward to working with Ken, but I'm sure Heath will be an equally good operator.'

'So good to hear you back to your old optimistic self, Phoebs. I'd love to chat and hear all about Heath, but I have to dash. The Underground waits for no one,' Susy said. 'Hope sonny-boy is not too nerdy or dull—but it's only for a few weeks. Talk tomorrow. I'll call you.'

With that, Suzy hung up.

Nerdy? *I wish…* Dull? *Not in anyone's book.* In fact she had to admit that Heath seemed perfect…if a little battle worn.


Heath arrived at the practice early the next morning. He had a surgical list beginning at one, with two post-operative patients and two new patients in the morning. Phoebe's day was light—three morning patients and two in the afternoon. Heath had arranged it that way to allow her to settle in.

Generally December was not busy, as most patients delayed non-urgent treatment, particularly surgery, until after the busy holiday season. By the time her patient numbers increased Heath knew he would be back in Sydney and his father would be back on deck.

'Good morning,' Tilly greeted her brother as she dropped her bag behind the desk. 'Loving the cool air in here.'

'It's great, isn't it? Not sure the landlord will be thrilled when he sees the invoice, but it's worth every penny.'

'*Dad* owns the building. *He's* the landlord.'

Heath laughed. 'Yes—and hopefully I'll be back in Sydney when he gets the bill in the mail. I had it completely overhauled and replaced the motor.'

'I think he can cover it.'

'Not sure about that, since he has the most expensive receptionist in the country.'

Tilly rolled her eyes and smiled. 'You're in fine form today, Heath. Be nice to your sister or I'll walk out—and then you'll be lost without my administrative wizardry.'

Heath headed back to his consulting room, and on the way checked that everything had been prepared for Phoebe. Her patient list was all in order. He had set up her log-in details for the computer and given her access to the database with the patient notes. The room was spotless. Although he refused to admit it to himself, he wanted to impress her.

'Hi, Phoebe,' Heath heard his sister say cheerily from the other end of the practice.

'Hi, Tilly,' Phoebe replied. She stepped inside, feeling apprehensive and nervous, as if it was the first day at school. 'It's a lot cooler than a couple of days ago in here.'

'Hopefully we can avoid doctors and patients fainting,' Heath said as he walked briskly down the corridor and into the waiting room.

'Good morning, Heath.'

'I'll show you to your consulting room.'

Phoebe could sense that he had slipped back into his cool demeanour again, but he wasn't quite as cold and she did not take it personally.

'I'll try not to faint on the way,' she said, in an attempt to lighten the mood.

Heath smirked, but because he was leading the way Phoebe didn't see. Her view was his broad shoulders, slim hips and the long stride he was taking. And, despite not wanting to notice, it was the best damn view she had seen in days. In fact the last time she had seen anything so impressive was in the very same man at the pool.

* * *

'Nancy Wilson?' Phoebe called into the waiting room.

A young woman stood up and followed Phoebe into her consulting room, hobbling a little and clearly in pain.

Phoebe closed the door. 'Let me introduce myself, Nancy. I'm Dr Phoebe Johnson and I've stepped in to help Dr Ken Rollins for the next few months. Please take a seat.' Phoebe had briefly read the patient's notes and was aware of her medical history of chronic heel pain. 'I see you have undergone some reconstructive treatments with Dr Rollins.'

'Yes, but it hasn't made a permanent improvement.'

'I see. Did you find any of them had long-lasting benefits? I know it was more invasive, but was the plasma therapy successful from your perspective? Or did you prefer the low-intensity shock wave treatment?'

'Both were good—but only short term. I'm an ice skater. I hope to compete for Australia in Switzerland in nine months, so I need to be back on my feet and out of pain to train in Europe and then compete. At the moment it feels like there's a pebble in my left shoe when I walk. On really bad days it's like a shard of glass.'

'They are common descriptions of the problem. Please come over to the examination table and I'll have a look,' Phoebe said, and assisted the young woman to the narrow table against the far wall. She moved a small step into place with her foot to help Nancy climb up onto the bed. 'I appreciate you've tried the conservative approach, and to be honest, Nancy, sometimes after all else fails there's no choice but to choose corrective surgical treatment.'

Phoebe eased the soft boot and sock from the woman's left foot and then, slipping on surgical gloves, began her examination. Although the conservative restorative treatments to increase blood flow and break up scar tissue had assisted temporarily with pain management, Phoebe decided that surgery was the only option.

'Unfortunately your plantar fasciitis has not improved with past treatments, and your ice skating training has, according to your notes, been compromised for a number of months now.'

'Yes, I do train, but only for short periods, and then I require ice, cortisone, and when all else fails codeine to manage the pain—and then I lie in bed for hours some days.'

'Heavy doses of pain relief or cortisone are not long-term options for anyone, but particularly not at your age, Nancy. Nor is being incapacitated in bed an option for an athlete. Your condition is almost epidemic in the United States, with one in ten people suffering from varying degrees of heel pain from scar tissue, and it appears this approach is no longer viable for you, considering your lifestyle. We'll need to proceed to the next level on your treatment plan, so you can move forward with your career.'

'Surgery is fine by me. I just want to get it over and finished and get back on my feet—literally.'

Phoebe gently put the sock and soft boot back on the young woman and helped her down from the examination table. She explained the risks of surgery, confirmed that Nancy was in general good health and a suitable patient for surgery, and then walked her out to the front desk for Tilly to make the hospital arrangements and for Nancy to sign the consent forms.

Heath had just seen off his first patient for the day, and was at the reception desk checking up on a late arrival.

'Were you part of the medical team assisting the disabled athletes at the international games last year?' Nancy asked Phoebe as they waited for Tilly to check the surgical roster at the Eastern Memorial, where Phoebe would be operating.

'Yes, I was—but how did you know? The games weren't held in Australia.'

'My older brother Jason's a weightlifter. He lives in Detroit with his wife and baby daughter,' Nancy continued as she offered Tilly her credit card for the consultation payment. 'He suffers from congenital amputation of his left leg below the knee, and he had a similar issue to me with his right heel the night before his heat. I remember he told me about a consultation he had with Dr Phoebe Johnson, the podiatric surgeon with the American team. Once I heard your accent I assumed that there couldn't be two of you in the same specialty.'

'No—not that I'm aware of anyway,' Phoebe replied as she finished signing the notes so Tilly could book surgery the following week. She turned back to Nancy. 'Being involved with the teams was a wonderful experience. Can you please give my best to Jason? If I remember correctly he won a medal—was it silver?'

'Yes, and he was thrilled to win it. He swore that if it wasn't for you and the treatment you provided to alleviate the pain he would have pulled out and wasted almost four years of training.'

Heath walked back to his office, unavoidably impressed with this experience that Phoebe had kept close to her chest and not put on her CV. She was even more unforthcoming than him!

He wondered what else he didn't know about his temporary associate. And he still wondered if this small inner-city practice would prove enough of a challenge for her...

The morning was steady, and by lunchtime Heath was preparing to leave for his afternoon surgical list at the Eastern Memorial. Aware that Phoebe's last patient for the morning had left, he knocked on the open door of Phoebe's consulting room.

'Come in, Tilly.'

Heath paused. 'It's not Tilly.'

Phoebe turned from her computer screen, where she was reading through the notes for her first afternoon patient.

'Sorry, Heath—come in.'

With only fifteen minutes before he had to leave for the hospital, he wanted to catch up and see how her morning had progressed. And he just wanted to see her but couldn't admit that even to himself.

Before he had a chance to open his mouth, Tilly knocked on the door.

'This time it has to be Tilly,' Phoebe remarked as she watched Heath cross his arms across his broad chest.

'Yep, you're running out of alternative suspects now.'

Phoebe smiled, then asked Tilly to join them.

'Sorry to interrupt, Phoebe, but your afternoon patients have both cancelled due to the extreme weather,' Tilly told her. 'So it looks like you've got the afternoon off.'

'Oh, no. That's disappointing,' Phoebe said, slumping into her chair and not masking her feelings. 'I feel so guilty, being here and doing nothing.' She had a strong work ethic and that made sitting around seem a complete waste of time for her and a waste of money for the practice. 'I've had more time off since I arrived than I've worked.'

Heath considered her for a moment and then came up with a suggestion. 'I have an idea to appease your misguided sense of guilt. Why don't you assist me in Theatre over at the Eastern Memorial this afternoon? I have three on the surgical list and I could do with an extra set of hands—but we'd need to leave immediately.'

Phoebe sat bolt-upright and answered with an unhesitating, 'Yes!' as she reached for her bag. 'Let's go…I'm all yours.'

Heath nodded, but his body abruptly reminded him that if his life had played out differently and Phoebe really was *all his* there would be far more pleasurable things he would do with her that afternoon.

# CHAPTER SEVEN

THE SCRUB NURSE greeted Heath as he prepared for the first patient.

'Abby, we have Phoebe Johnson, a podiatric surgeon from Washington, joining us this afternoon,' Heath announced as he turned off the tap with his foot and shook the water from his hands into the scrub room trough.

'Hi, Phoebe, welcome aboard.'

'Pleased to meet you, Abby.'

Phoebe slipped her freshly scrubbed hands inside some surgical gloves. Her long dark hair was in a flat bun and neatly secured inside a floral cap, and like the other two she was already dressed in sterile blue scrubs. They entered the theatre just as the patient was drifting off under anaesthesia.

'So, today's patient is a thirty-five-year-old professional skateboarder. He's here for a lateral ankle ligament reconstruction. The ankle has not responded to non-surgical treatment and has been unstable for over six months,' Heath informed the surgical team, including two observing third-year medical students as he began marking the stained sterile area. 'Would you like to lead on this one, Phoebe?'

Phoebe was both flattered and pleased to be asked.

Heath was a complex man, but a man who treated her as his equal, not only in words but in actions.

Quietly she declined. 'I'd prefer to assist today. We can switch it around another time, perhaps.'

'Certainly.' Heath looked over his surgical mask at Phoebe for slightly longer than required before he averted his eyes back to the patient. 'I routinely use the modified Brostrom procedure.' He confidently made a J-shaped incision over the outside of the patient's left ankle with his scalpel, identified the ankle ligaments and began the process of tightening them, using anchors that he placed on to the fibula bone.

Phoebe appreciated the way he led the students through the procedure by describing the steps clearly and precisely.

'I'm stitching other tissue over the repaired ligaments to further strengthen the repair,' he said as he continued, with Phoebe holding the incision open with forceps.

Phoebe had done many of these operations over the years. 'That looks great, Heath. Very clean and tidy. I've had a few when I've needed to use tendons to replace the ligaments. I've woven a tendon into the bones around the ankle and held it in place with stitches, and occasionally a screw in the bone. I've utilised a patient's own hamstring tendon before. But it made it a much longer operation as I had to take the hamstring tendon through a separate incision on the inside part of the knee.'

Heath nodded in agreement. 'On more than one occasion I've needed to use a cadaver tendon and had to weave it into the fibula bone. There's many ways to solve a problem like this, and as we know each has its merits.'

Phoebe and Heath worked together as if they had been operating as a team for years—or at the very least months. Their effortless collaboration would be deceptive to any external observers, who might not think that this was their first time together in the operating theatre. Phoebe was able to pre-empt Heath's next move, and neither of them could deny their natural synchronisation.

'That went well.'

Phoebe nodded her agreement with Heath's statement as they scrubbed in for the second operation. Each was exceptionally happy with how well they'd worked together but not wanting to state the obvious.

They made a great team.

The afternoon progressed well, with the other two patients' procedures completed successfully and on time. Phoebe felt a great deal of satisfaction working with such a skilful surgeon as Heath. His dexterity and knowledge in the field was second to none and, while she was confident in her own abilities, she felt there was still much she could learn from him.

After only a short time in the operating theatre with Heath she could see that he had a level of skill that must come close to his father's. The knowledge Heath had casually and without ceremony imparted to her already was amazing, and she was excited for the next few weeks until he left for Sydney.

'I really hope we can do this again.' The words rushed from her lips with unbridled honesty as she removed her surgical gloves and cap.

Heath watched as her long dark hair tumbled free and fell over her shoulders. In the harsh theatre lights she still looked gorgeous, and he knew that in any lighting her stunning smile and sparkling eyes would bring a glow to the room.

'I'd like that,' he said, and again kept his eyes focused on her for a little longer than a casual glance.

Phoebe flinched and felt something tug at her heart.

Was it pity for the man? Or desire? She wasn't sure, but there was something stirring inside.

'Would you like to grab some dinner? My way to say thank you for assisting in there this afternoon.'

Heath had surprised himself with the invitation, but he enjoyed spending time with Phoebe and it seemed a natural progression for the day. They had a professional connection, and he told himself it was nothing more than a dinner invitation to a colleague.

'I'll have to go out and eat anyway. Oscar will be eating at Tilly's, and Dad will more than likely defrost a TV dinner, so I will need to pick up something or eat alone at a restaurant. You'll be doing me a favour by sharing a table with me.'

'If you put it that way...' she replied.

'That's settled, then,' Heath said as he left to change into his street clothes. 'As you know, I have your address, so what say I pick you up at seven?'

'Sounds perfect.'

'I'll put Oscar to bed early, since last night was a late one for him, then you and I can have a nice dinner somewhere—maybe even in the foothills. I'll show you something of Adelaide. It should be a little cooler out tonight, so I'll find a good alfresco restaurant.'

Phoebe walked into the female change room. There were two other young doctors also changing from their scrubs to day clothes, but they didn't notice Phoebe and continued their conversation.

'Did you know he's back in town?' an attractive redhead asked the other woman. 'He's been here for a week already.'

'The doctor with the *no second date* rule?' the blonde doctor replied as she ran a brush though her short bobbed hair, then put it back on the shelf and closed her locker. 'Yes, I heard he came back last week and that he's here for a month.'

'I wonder how many hearts he'll break in that time, with his hard and fast rules. And don't forget the *never meet his son* rule. There was another one too, but I can't think of it now.'

'I think it's to *leave before the sun comes up.*'

'That's right. Pity he's so damned gorgeous—if he wasn't he'd never get away with it.'

They both slammed shut their lockers. 'But despite all that he doesn't hide the rules. I hear he's upfront with all the women he intends to bed. They all know what they're getting into and not one has ever met his precious son. Dr Rollins is a player, but he's an honest one.'

Almost two hours later there was a knock on Phoebe's front door.

Thank God, she thought as she sprayed a light fragrance on her neck and wrists, that this wasn't really a date. It had the makings of a date, and to others observing it might even look like a date, but to Phoebe it most certainly *wasn't* a date. She wasn't ready for anything close to a date. And after what she'd heard in the locker room she never would be. They would only ever be friends— because she had already met his son, so clearly he wasn't thinking about bedding her.

Deep in thought, she smoothed her hands over her long white summer dress as she made her way from her room. The halter-style dress, cinched at the waist by a thin gold belt, was made of soft cotton that flowed as she moved. She wore simple flat gold sandals to match. Her hair fell in silky curls around her bare shoulders.

'Hi, Phoebe,' Heath greeted her as she opened the door.

'Hi, Heath. Let me grab my bag and I'll be right with you.' She picked up her purse and keys and locked the door behind her as they left.

'It's a little cooler this evening, like I predicted, so I've left the top down to enjoy the fresh air on the drive but if you'd prefer I can put it up again.'

Phoebe looked past him to see his silver convertible sports car parked by her front gate. Then her gaze quickly returned to him. His white T-shirt was snug across his toned chest and he wore khaki trousers. A single, handsome medic with a sports car would be every woman's dream. But not hers—not after what she'd heard.

She reached into her purse for a hair tie. 'You can leave the top down,' she said and she pulled her hair into a high ponytail.

Heath had to remind himself that he was doing the right thing and providing dinner for a colleague who had done a great job in Theatre that afternoon. And not that she was a woman whose company he was very much beginning to enjoy.

'So, I thought we'd head up to Hahndorf for dinner. It's a German town in the Adelaide Hills.'

'Sounds lovely,' she said as they walked to his car.

Heath held open the car door and, after lifting the flowing hem of her dress safely inside, closed and patted it, as if he had secured precious cargo. It did not go unnoticed by Phoebe and it made her feel torn—almost like jumping back out and telling him that it was a mistake and she wasn't hungry.

The car suddenly felt a little like a sports version of a fairytale carriage, and she was *not* looking for Prince Charming—and by reputation he was far from that gallant. But he was in the car and the engine was running before she could muster an excuse.

'Hahndorf—is that how you say it?'

'Yes,' he said, and moments later had pulled away from the kerb and into the traffic. 'It's about twenty minutes up the freeway. Something different—I hope you like it.'

As he said this he turned momentarily to see Phoebe look back at him with her warm brown eyes. She was a conundrum. He sensed so many layers to the woman who sat beside him, and one layer appeared to be a lack of trust. He wondered why. What had caused Phoebe to be outwardly happy and yet as distant as himself on a personal level?

Except around his son. She seemed to let her guard down around him very easily.

Had her heart been broken? he wondered as he entered the freeway and picked up speed.

The drive in the warm evening air was wonderful and their chatter was intermittent as Phoebe admired the scenery of the foothills.

'It was a pity you didn't bring our work to Tilly's the other morning. We could have gone over the patient notes by the pool,' Phoebe suddenly announced as he slowed a little to take the turn-off to Hahndorf.

Guilt slammed into Heath. 'I thought it would be easier at the office,' he said, clearing his throat. He had to keep it simple, when in fact it was so far from that.

Phoebe surveyed the scenery, dotted with massive gum trees that enveloped them as they drove into the quaint town. This evening would be a no-strings-attached walk in the park—or in this case a walk in a German town.

'I'm looking forward to visiting this town and to eating authentic German cuisine. I've never had the opportunity to travel to Germany—or the time, to be honest—so this is my chance to sample it.'

Heath pulled into a restaurant car park. The breeze had

picked up but there were no rain clouds, so he left the top of his car down. 'There are great reviews about the food here, although I've not been. Tilly says it's very nice.'

Heath looked down at his watch. Their dinner reservation was not until seven forty-five, so they had fifteen minutes to spare.

'Would you like to walk for a few minutes? Take in the sights of the town? It's not quite the size of New York, so fifteen minutes should have it covered.'

Phoebe turned to catch what she thought was a smile from Heath.

They walked along the narrow footpath and stepped inside the small antiquity shops still open for the tourist trade and window-shopped at those that had closed.

Heath was enjoying the time with Phoebe.

'I think we can head back to the restaurant, if you're ready,' he told her as they stepped from a bric-a-brac shop where Phoebe had been admiring the vintage hand-embroidered tablecloths and runners. 'The sauerkraut is probably primed to go.'

Phoebe laughed and followed his lead to the casual eatery, where the *maître d'* showed them to a table outside and provided them with menus. There were lights strung up high across the alfresco dining area, and their small table had a lovely street view. She felt more relaxed the more she thought of Heath as a colleague. A very handsome colleague, who bedded other women but would never bed her.

'I love that all the speciality dishes are served with creamy mustard potato bake, sauerkraut, red wine sauce and German mustard. It seems so authentic. Hahndorf really is Adelaide's little Germany,' Phoebe said as she looked over the menu.

Heath ordered a crisp white wine and some iced water while Phoebe tried to focus on the menu. It all looked wonderful, and there was a varied selection within the list of traditional German fare. Her mouth twisted a little from side to side as she carefully considered her options. Her finger softly tapped her bottom lip as she weighed up her decision.

Heath fell a little further under the spell she didn't know she was casting—one he was finding it almost futile to ignore.

'I think...' She paused to reread, and then continued. 'I think I would like the smoked Kassler chops, please.'

'Sounds great. I'll go with the Schweinshaxe—crispy skin pork hock is a favourite of mine.'

With that he signalled the waiter and placed their order. The waiter returned moments later with the drinks, before leaving them alone again.

Phoebe was staring at the people walking by and at the cars slowly moving down the single-lane road that meandered through the town. She was thinking about Washington, covered in snow, while she was enjoying a balmy evening in the foothills on the other side of the world.

'A penny for your thoughts?'

'It will cost you a quarter.'

'A quarter of what?'

'A quarter of a dollar.'

Heath rubbed the cleft in his chin and considered her terms. 'Tell me honestly—are your thoughts right now worth twenty-five cents?'

'I guess unless you pay up you'll never know,' Phoebe returned with a cheeky smile.

Heath decided to call her bluff and, reaching for his wallet, found a twenty-cent and a five-cent coin. He placed both on the table and pushed them towards her with lean strong fingers. 'Well, your thoughts are officially mine now.'

'I was thinking about Washington...'

'International thoughts are always more expensive, so I can see why there was a price-hike from a penny to twenty-five cents,' he teased. 'So go on.'

Phoebe bit the inside of her lip. 'That's it.'

*'That's it?'*

'Yep. I'm afraid you probably didn't get your money's worth after all,' Phoebe said with her head at a tilt. 'It was always going to be a gamble. When the stakes are high and you play big...sometimes you lose.'

Heath's lips curved a little at her response. He suddenly had the feeling that spending time with Phoebe would never be a loss.


'That was delicious—thank you so much.'

'You're most welcome,' he replied as they made their way along the now darkened street.

Street lamps lit their way, but the sky was dark and dotted with sparkling stars. The breeze had picked up a little over the almost two hours they had spent eating and conversing, but it was refreshing, not cold, and it carried along with it the gentle wafts of eucalyptus and other native bushes.

Phoebe filled her lungs with the beautiful fresh air. Both had purposely steered the conversation away from their personal lives and discussed issues aligned to their careers.

'We can head to my father's home, if you like, to have a coffee with him.' Heath wanted to prolong his time with Phoebe, but in a way that was safe for both of them.

'Isn't it a bit late to be calling on your father?' she asked as they left the freeway and headed towards the city residence.

'My father is a night owl. He has been for many years. He was always the last to bed. I remember coming home in the early hours of the morning sometimes, maybe from a pub crawl with uni friends, and he would still be up reading.'

'And your mother didn't mind?'

Heath drew a shallow breath. Although it had been a long time since his mother had died he still felt the loss.

'My mother was killed in a light plane crash returning from Kangaroo Island. She was a social worker and had been over there consulting about issues with the high rate of school truancy. She was working on strategies to keep the children on the island engaged, and she called my father just before she boarded, very excited with the outcome. She told him that they had made significant progress and that she would tell him all about it when she arrived home. The plane went down ten minutes after take-off from Kingscote, in bad weather that had come in quickly.'

'I'm so sorry to hear that.' Phoebe's hand instinctively covered her mouth for a moment. She felt her heart sink with the news he had just broken. That meant he had lost two women he had loved. That was a heavy burden to carry for any man.

'How old were you at the time, Heath?'

'Sixteen—so it will be twenty years this July since she was killed.'

The desolate expression on Phoebe's face told Heath how she was feeling. She knew she had no words that could capture the depth of his sadness so she didn't try to speak.

'I think, to be honest, he has no reason to go to bed early any more. There's no one waiting so he stays up late—unless he has an early surgery roster...then he goes to bed at a reasonable hour.'

'And he's never wanted to remarry?'

'No. He and my mother were soul mates. He didn't think he would find that again, so he never looked.'

'That's sad. There might have been someone just perfect...' Phoebe replied—then realised that she was overstepping the mark, by commenting about someone else's love-life when her own had been a disaster, and stopped.

'Perhaps. But he's never recovered from losing my mother. Some people never do. They just can't move on.'

Phoebe wondered if Heath was the same as his father. Cut from the same cloth and faithful to the woman he had lost. Never having healed enough to be with someone else.

They travelled along in silence after that, until Heath pulled up at the front of the beautiful old sandstone villa that his father had called home for so many years, and where he was staying for just a few weeks. Standard white roses, eight bushes on each side, lined the pathway.

Someone must have been watering them in the extreme weather, Phoebe mused as she walked past them, tempted to touch the perfect white petals. Their delicate perfume hung in the night air. The front porch light was on and the home had a welcoming feel to it. It was as if there was a woman still living there, Phoebe thought as she made her way to the front door with Heath.

He unlocked it and they both stepped inside.

'Hi, Dad, we're home. I hope you're decent. I have Phoebe with me, and you don't need to scare her in your underwear, or worse.'

Phoebe felt a smile coming on at the humour in his greeting and it lifted her spirits. She looked around and was very taken by the beautiful stained glass around the door of the softly lit entrance hall. And she felt comforted by the lighthearted side of their father-son relationship. It was not unlike the way she related to her own father. The warmth, respect and humorous rapport were very similar.

'I'm outside on the patio.'

Heath dropped his keys onto the antique hall stand and

then led the way down the long hallway, through the huge country-style kitchen, complete with pots and pans over-hanging the marble cooking island, to the back veranda. From what she could see of the house in the dim lighting it was pristine, and she wondered if it was the work of Ken or if perhaps he had a cleaning service to keep it looking so picture-perfect. It didn't look like two men were living there.

Phoebe excused herself to visit the bathroom while Heath walked through the French doors to the patio.

'There you are,' he said to his father, who was sitting in the light of the moon.

'Yes, just sitting alone with my thoughts. And here's one of them. Don't look at me as a role model—look at me as a warning... It's not a real life without a woman to share it. Don't leave it too long to look for love again.'

# CHAPTER EIGHT

THE NEXT DAY Phoebe was sitting in the cool of her house. It was the weekend, and the previous days had gone by quickly. She had been busy consulting at the practice, but she was a little disappointed that the opportunity to operate with Heath had not arisen again. The way they had preempted each other's needs during surgery still remained in her mind and she looked forward to the opportunity to do it again.

Heath had been at the hospital, presenting some tutorials for the third-year medical students, but they'd caught up at the practice briefly, and talked over any questions that Phoebe had had about her patients. She had reminded herself that with his *rules* they would never be more than friends, but despite her still simmering feelings that she needed to ignore, he was still a fascinating friend to have.

Phoebe was enjoying her work, but the jet-lag had finally caught up with her and she'd wanted to have plenty of rest to ensure she didn't compromise her patients, so she had enjoyed a couple of early nights.

Wondering what to do on a Saturday, she put on a load of washing, did some yoga and although she considered calling her father, it was still Friday in the US. No doubt he would be busy, dealing with some political emergency, so she decided to leave it until the end of his day—which would be just after lunch for her. She didn't dare call her mother, to hear yet another sales pitch about her repentant ex-fiancé, so she decided not to make any calls.

It was much too hot to head to the park or the Botanic Gardens so, while the washing was on its spin cycle, she picked up a magazine that she had purchased at the airport and left on the coffee table and thought perhaps later she would visit the museum or an art gallery.

Suddenly the doorbell rang. With a puzzled expression she looked through the window to see a delivery truck parked outside her home. She tentatively opened the door. Surely there wouldn't be another delivery? It would be the second since she'd arrived in town.

'Phoebe Johnson?'

'Yes.'

'Great,' the man replied, lifting his baseball cap slightly and handing her an electronic device with a signature pad. 'I have a delivery for you. Sign here, love, and I'll bring it in.'

Phoebe signed, then watched as the man disappeared back to his truck. He opened the large double doors and stepped up inside. There were some loud banging and dragging sounds coming from the back of the truck and Phoebe's brows knitted in confusion. She had no clue who would be sending her something. And how big *was* this delivery?

Suddenly the delivery man emerged and jumped down from the truck. He pulled a huge box out onto the road. Then another two smaller packages. He also pulled down a trolley, and piled everything on top and headed back in Phoebe's direction.

'Are you sure all of that is for me?'

'Dead sure, love,' he said, as he waited for her to step aside so he could wheel it inside.

Phoebe followed him and told him to leave it to the side of the living room, near the kitchen doorway. He offloaded all the items and then left, closing the front door behind him.

Phoebe scratched her head as she searched for the delivery note and discovered it was from a local department store. She headed into the kitchen, found some scissors and began to cut open the largest of the three packages.

A moment later she squealed in delight. It was a Christmas tree. But as she pulled it gently from the oversized box she could see it was a very special type of tree.

The branches were the deepest forest-green, and looked so real. She moved closer and smiled as she could smell pinecones. It was just like the tree she'd had back home when she was very young. It was still her favourite Christmas tree of all time, and she had looked forward every year to her mother and father bringing it down from the attic and spending the night decorating it, with tinsel and lights, and baubles with their names handwritten on them in gold. Even the dog had had a personalised bauble...

But the branches had broken one by one over the years, and eventually the tree had had to be replaced. They hadn't been able to find the same one. And the new one had been nice but it was a slightly different green and it didn't smell like pinecones. It just hadn't been the same...

She heard her phone ringing in the other room and raced to pick it up.

'Do you like it?' the very recognisable voice asked. 'I asked them to text me when they'd delivered it. In the catalogue it looked like the one we had when you were a little girl.'

'It is—it's just the same! Thank you so much, Dad. I love it, and it was so sweet of you.'

'Well, I couldn't have my little girl the other side of the

world and all alone for her favourite time of the year without a tree,' he told her.

'But there are two more boxes.'

'You can't have a tree without decorations.'

Phoebe felt a tear trickle down her cheek. 'I miss you.'

'Miss you more—but I have to head back in to deal with another crisis. Middle East is on the agenda again today,' he said, then added, 'I want to hear all about work and your new home. I'll call you again soon.'

'Thank you again, Dad. Love you!'

'Ditto, sweetie.'

Phoebe had planned on putting up her Christmas tree that night, but she got a call from Tilly, inviting her to dinner. It was Ken's birthday.

They were such a social family, and it was stopping her from feeling lonely, so she accepted. It meant spending time with Heath but she hoped that with the family around and by catching yet another cab, she would keep that professional distance between them. But as it was Ken's birthday she realised she would need to race into the city for a gift.

She closed the giant box and dragged it across the polished floorboards into the second bedroom, and then put the boxes of decorations in with it. She looked forward to putting it up another day.

As she closed the door she felt a little ache inside. This should have been her first Christmas with Giles, in their own home as husband and wife. She didn't miss him, but she still felt sad that she was spending it so far from home.

The birthday dinner was lovely. It was the whole family again, and Ken loved the astronomy book Phoebe gave him. Heath was pleasant, but he seemed a little preoccupied as he sat at the end of the table with Oscar by his side.

Knowing what she did about his past, she didn't press him to be anything more than he could be, but she enjoyed his company and found that during the evening that he seemed to grow less guarded, and even smiled once or twice at her stories of growing up in the US. And she managed, with a concerted effort, to keep her butterflies at bay.

The next few days sped by. The weather had thankfully cooled slightly—enough that Phoebe felt the need for a light sweater one night. She had planned on putting up the tree over the weekend, but on Sunday she had slept in and read some patient notes to prepare for Monday's surgical schedule, so it was still packed away.

Ken invited her over on Wednesday for 'hump day takeout'. This time it was just the four of them. And that night Heath took the seat next to her.

Oscar smiled at his grandpa.

And his grandpa hoped Heath was taking his advice on board.

They chatted about work, and then about their lives outside of work. The conversation between Heath and Phoebe continued on the patio as a light breeze picked up and Oscar was tucked up in bed.

'Does it feel like second nature, being in Adelaide now?' he asked.

'It does. In fact this whole experience is strange in that it feels almost like déjà-vu in familiarity. Your family are wonderful—so down-to-earth and welcoming.'

Phoebe looked out across the garden from the wicker chair where she sat. The landscaping wasn't modern and manicured, like Tilly's, it was more like a scene from *The Secret Garden.* The flowerbeds were overflowing with floral ground cover, large old trees with low-hanging branches lined the perimeter of the generous-sized property, and there was an uneven clay brick pathway leading to an archway covered in jasmine.

It was beautiful and timeless and she felt so very much at home in Ken's house. All that was missing, she thought, was a Christmas tree and a hearth in the living room. The hearth would never happen in temperatures over one hundred degrees, but perhaps she could work on bringing a little bit of Christmas to the three men who lived there.

'My family have their moments,' Heath told her.

'Don't they all? But yours don't appear to interfere in your life, which is great.'

Heath shook his head. 'Believe me, they try—but I put a stop to it quickly.' Then he paused. 'The way you said that sounded a little Freudian. Am I to gather that your family *does*?'

Phoebe ran her hand along the balustrade next to her. 'Sometimes.'

Heath sat down in the armchair next to hers. 'Did they try to interfere in your decision to come to Australia?'

Phoebe rolled her eyes and sipped her soda and lime as she recalled the last conversation she'd had with her mother, by the waiting cab.

'I'm taking your expression to be a yes,' Heath commented.

'Well, a yes to my mother—but my father was supportive from the get-go,' she said, putting the glass down on the table.

'Why was that?'

'He knew I needed a break from Washington and he wanted to help.'

'But your mother didn't think you needed a break?'

'Hardly…' she lamented. 'She wanted me to stay and work it out.' Phoebe instantly realised that she had said too much, but the words were already out.

'Work what out?' he asked, leaning forward in the chair with a perplexed look on his face.

'Oh, just things… You know—things that she thought needed to be worked through and I thought needed to be walked away from.'

'No, I can't say I do know what you mean, Phoebe.'

She sighed. She knew she had to elaborate, but she had no intention of going into all of the detail. 'Relationship issues. Some of those just can't be sorted out.'

'With another family member?'

'No, thank God—he never made it into the family.'

'Ah…so an issue with a man, then?'

'Yes, with a man.'

'So you ran away to the colonies of Australia to get away from a man?"

'Uh-huh…' she mumbled, and then, looking at the question dressing his very handsome face, she continued, 'Now you know everything there is to know about me, it's your turn. What is Heath Rollins's story? Have *you* ever run away from anything?'

As she said it she wanted to kick herself. She knew his story, and it was a sad one that begged not to be retold. He had lost both his mother and his wife. And Phoebe suddenly felt like the most insensitive woman in the world to be asking that question.

'I'm sorry, I shouldn't have asked. Please ignore me.'

Heath considered her expression for a moment. There was sadness in her face, almost pity. 'You know about my wife?'

'Yes.'

'Well, you know I did run away from something, then. From overwhelming grief and a gaping hole so big that I never thought it would heal.'

She closed her eyes for a moment. 'I can't begin to know what that feels like.'

He sat back in his chair again in silence, with memories rushing to the fore. 'Did my father let you know or was it Tilly?' His voice was calm—not accusing, but sombre.

'Neither,' she answered honestly. 'It was Oscar. He told me the other day, when we were in the garden at Tilly's. He said that he was very little when his mother died and doesn't remember anything. I assume he must have been a toddler.'

Heath was surprised that Oscar had opened up about it to Phoebe. He rarely spoke of his mother, and particularly not to anyone he didn't really know.

'He was five months old, actually—when Natasha died. He never had the chance to know his mother. To walk beside her or even to hold her hand.'

'Oh…I don't know what to say except that I'm so sorry, Heath.' As she sat on the chair next to him she felt her heart breaking for him. 'After a loss as devastating as that it must have been so hard for you to even begin to find your way through the grief and cope for the sake of your son.'

'It was hard for all of us, watching her die. Knowing there was nothing we could do. It was the hardest time of my life and I was powerless to stop it. I felt guilty for allowing it to happen, for not making her have treatment earlier.'

Phoebe didn't ask what had taken his wife's life. It wasn't for her to know. But she could see he was still wearing the guilt. 'You can't make a person do what you want if it's not their wish. They have to do what is right for them, even if it's not what we see as right. I'm sure she had her reasons for not starting treatment.'

'Yes—Oscar was the reason. She was twenty weeks pregnant when Stage Three breast cancer was diagnosed, and although she could have safely undergone modified chemotherapy during the pregnancy she refused. She wanted to wait until she had given birth, then start the treatment but with the hormones surging through her body she understood there was a chance it would spread. But it was a risk she wanted to take. In my mind, with the oncologist's advice, it was one she never needed to even consider. They took Oscar four weeks early, but the cancer had already metastasised. She underwent surgery and chemo but she knew it was useless. She had done her research and was aware that there was little chance of her surviving.'

'What an amazingly selfless woman.'

'More than you can know. But at the time I was angry with her, for leaving me with a baby to raise and no wife to love.'

Phoebe watched Heath wringing his hands in frustration.

'I can understand your feelings, but I guess I can also understand your wife had a right to do what she thought was best. Sometimes what two people in love want is not the same, and it's not that either is wrong, or not respecting the other, it's just that they see things differently. Their life experience and values alter their perspective. And she was a mother. I can't say it from any experience, since I have never had a child, but I am sure carrying a baby would change everything about how you see the world.'

'But she was so young, and she had so much to live for—no matter how I try I will never understand. I love Oscar so much, and I'm grateful every day for him being in my life, but it was a huge and difficult choice she had to make. And I feel guilty for what happened because it means Oscar is growing up without a mother.'

Phoebe was puzzled at his feelings of remorse. She understood the sadness, but not the guilt. 'I don't know why you would say that. Your wife made the decision—not you.'

'But I should have made her have the chemo. I should have never let her delay it. And perhaps I shouldn't have married her so young. If she hadn't married me then she wouldn't have rushed into having a child, and when she was diagnosed she would have gone ahead with treatment.'

'Heath, you can't know that for sure. Natasha might not have been diagnosed until it was too late anyway. A young woman in her twenties wouldn't have been having mammograms, so it might have gone undetected for a long time—by which time she might have faced the same fate. It's something you will never know. But you have a very special little boy. And you can't harbour any blame—it's not good for Oscar.'

Heath nodded, but Phoebe could see his thoughts were somewhere else, struggling with his memories.

He was thinking back to the day Natasha had died.

It had been Christmas Day.

The next day Phoebe woke early, still thinking about everything that Heath had told her. While the heartbreak Giles had inflicted on her had been soul-destroying at the time, she knew now that it had been for the best. But nothing about Heath's heartbreak was for the best. His wife had died and left behind a little boy who would never know her. And a man who couldn't fully understand or accept her reasons.

She felt a little homesick for the first time, and called her father.

'I assisted in surgery last week, and I'm heading in today to the practice, and then tomorrow I'm in Theatre again,' she told him as she ate her muesli and fruit breakfast with her mobile phone on speaker. 'And I finally met Ken Rollins.'

'That's great. I bet you quizzed him about his papers.'

'I did and he was so generous with his knowledge.'

'How long will his son be filling in before he leaves and heads back to his old position?'

Phoebe's mood suddenly and unexpectedly fell as she listened to her father and was reminded that Heath and Oscar were only transient in her life. She had enjoyed spending time with Heath out of work hours. No matter how much she was looking forward to working with Ken, she knew she would miss Heath. He was charming company when he lifted his guard, and he had managed to make her feel important with the way he listened to her and engaged in their conversations.

He was a far cry from the distracted man who had once held the title of her fiancé. And she suddenly felt a little sad that Heath would be gone in a few short weeks. She knew she wanted more. What that was, she wasn't sure—but she knew even after such a short time there would be a void in her life when he left.

'Um…I'm not sure, exactly,' she muttered, trying not to think about exactly how much she would miss him as she washed her bowl and spoon and put them in the dish drainer. 'I think another four weeks, unless Ken's recovery takes longer.'

Phoebe realised she wouldn't be disappointed in any way if the older Dr Rollins chose to recuperate at home for a little longer than originally planned. She would be

more than agreeable to holding down the fort with his son.
In fact she knew it was something she wanted very much.

But that was in the hands of the universe and Ken's
doctor.

'Well, I miss you, honey, and so does your mother.'

'Miss you too, Dad. How is Mom?'

'Rushing about, keeping herself busy with her charity
work as always.'

'Maybe you could both head over for a short vacation
in sunny Australia in a few months? By then I will know
my way around and I can be your tour guide.'

'That sounds like a wonderful idea—but don't book any
accommodation for us yet. With the presidential election
only eleven months away I can't see sleep on my agenda,
let alone a vacation any time soon.'

'Of course—how silly of me. I guess I was caught up
with my life here and I forgot about everything happening back in Washington.'

'And that's a *good* thing. I'm proud of you, honey, and
you deserve this time away. Just don't come home with
an Australian drawl or I'll need to hire an interpreter!'

He laughed, then said goodbye, promising to call again
that week, and left Phoebe free to get ready for work.

The morning was filled with a few post-operative checks
and one new patient.

Phoebe loved working with Tilly. She was funny and
sweet and made the workplace even more enjoyable. And
she made her feel almost like part of the family.

She just wished that there was a way she could make
Heath feel whole again. But she doubted it. And she had
limited time. His guilt was not allowing him to move on.
Perhaps it also framed his *rules*. For those rules would protect him from getting too close to a woman again.

'Evan Jones?' she called, to the man she assumed was her next patient.

'That'd be me.'

The man in his early thirties stood, and with a strained expression on his suntanned face, using crutches, he crossed the room to Phoebe.

'We can take it slowly,' she said as they walked the short distance to her consulting room.

As she passed Heath's room she felt compelled to look, even though she knew he wasn't there. He hadn't been in all day. He had ward rounds at the hospital, then a short surgical roster to keep him occupied at the Eastern Memorial. She missed seeing his face, and wanted to believe that their current working arrangement could remain in place for a longer time.

Heath was everything she wanted in a colleague, a mentor and a friend. And perhaps even a lover, her body told her, before she quickly brought herself back to the task at hand. She should not be thinking about anything other than work. And definitely not thinking about Heath Rollins.

'Is that an American accent?' the man asked.

'Yes, East Coast,' she told him. 'Washington DC to be precise.'

He hobbled to the chair and rested his crutches against the nearby wall as Phoebe closed the door behind him. His patient notes told her that he was thirty-three years of age, a smoker and had suffered a heel fracture as a result of a fall from a balcony at a party. Without wanting to pass judgement, she couldn't help but wonder if alcohol had been a catalyst for the injury.

'So, Evan, your referring doctor has noted that the fall took place one week ago and that the CT scan she requested has confirmed you have a fractured calcaneus— or, more simply put, a broken heel bone.'

'Yes, my doc said that I smashed it when I fell from Bazza's ledge at 'is bucks' night.'

'It must have been quite the party. When's the wedding?'

'In two weeks. We've been like best mates for ever, and I'm meant to be 'is best man, but I'm gonna give it a miss 'cos I can't get across the sand for the wedding. It's on the beach at Noarlunga. That's what 'is missus wants. So I gotta just watch from the road.'

Phoebe nodded. She had no idea where Noarlunga was, and she was struggling a little with his heavy accent and wasn't too sure she had understood everything, but she knew she would be able to clarify the details during her examination. What she *did* know for a fact was that a best man on crutches, sinking into the sand, would not auger well for a romantic beach wedding, so she silently agreed with the bride's decision.

'Well, let me look at your injury and see if I can at least get you mobile enough to be in the audience—even if it is standing on the side of the road.'

Phoebe slipped the X-rays and the CT scan on the illuminated viewer, switched it on and then donned a pair of disposable gloves while she studied the films. The specific nature of the injury was leading her to concur with the referring doctor that surgery would be Evan's best option.

Kneeling down, she removed his moon boot and began to assess the damage done to his foot during the fall. 'I will chat to you in a moment, Evan, about our options to restore function and minimise pain.'

'Yeah, I'm throwing back painkillers like I got shares in the company.'

'We don't want you to be doing that for any extended period, so let's find a solution,' she replied as she gently elevated his foot. 'Does that hurt?'

'Nah—but I just tossed back a couple of strong ones about ten minutes ago, so ya could probably remove me kidney and I wouldn't feel a thing.'

Phoebe smiled. She still hadn't caught everything, but understood enough to see the humour in his remark. Evan's was the thickest Australian accent she had ever heard, and she guessed he was a not a city dweller. Well, at least had not always been a city dweller.

'Did you grow up in Adelaide, Evan?'

'Nah, I'm from up north. Grew up just outta Woomera, on a sheep station.'

'I'm guessing that would have been pretty dry and hot. Does it get hotter up there than here?'

Evan laughed. 'This isn't *hot*, Doc. Hot's when it's fifty in the shade—or, as you folks would say, about a hundred and twenty degrees.'

'Oh, my goodness. I can't imagine being that hot. I think I would die.'

'Plenty do, if they're not bush-savvy,' he replied with a grin. Then, as she lowered his foot to the ground, he grunted with the pain. 'That did hurt a bit.'

'I apologise, but I just had to check if the skin on your heel is wrinkled—this tells me the swelling has subsided sufficiently to proceed with surgery.'

'No worries. So I'm good to go out there and make a time for the surgery, then?'

'Not so quickly, Evan...' Phoebe removed her gloves and disposed of them in the bin before she took a seat and began reading the referral notes, along with the patient details he had completed for Tilly. 'At your age, and with the extent of the damage that is indicated on the X-rays, I think you're a good candidate for surgery, but I can see here that you wrote down that you're a smoker.'

'Yep, but I can hold off before the surgery, and even a

few hours afterwards. I've cut back heaps on 'em lately. What with the cost and all, it's sendin' me broke.'

'Actually, Evan,' Phoebe continued, looking directly at him with a serious expression on her face, 'you have to quit. Cold turkey, with no soft lead-in time, if we're to complete this in time for you to even be up and around to view the wedding from the side of the road.'

'Why?'

'Because smoking is harmful for wound and fracture-healing. I won't, in good conscience as a surgeon, consider you for surgery unless you stop smoking today.'

'That's a bit harsh, isn't it?'

'Unfortunately, Evan, I can't be gentle if you want me to operate and not compromise your health further. I need your vascular system at its peak to ensure the best results.'

'So say I give up—and I'm just puttin' it out there…not sayin' yet that I *will* give up—but say I do, when will you be operatin' and whatcha gonna do to me foot?'

'I could schedule the operation for approximately ten days from today. The procedure involves cutting through the skin to put the bone back together and using plates and screws to hold the alignment. It's called an open procedure and it involves an incision over the heel. The incision can be likened to a hockey stick, or a large L, where the overlying nerve and tendons are moved out of the way. The fracture fragments are restored to the best possible position. Then I will place a plate and screws to hold the fracture in place.'

Evan shifted uncomfortably in his seat. 'Makes me shiver all ovah. So I'll be right under while ya doin' it?'

'If you mean under general anaesthesia—yes. You will be in hospital and asleep during surgery. We will also use a regional nerve block, which involves a local injection to help with pain control. This block will provide between twelve and twenty-four hours of pain control after surgery. Surgery can be a same-day procedure, or planned with a hospital stay.'

'So will I have a moon boot again afterwards?'

'Post-surgical dressings and a splint or cast will be applied, and you won't be able to put weight on your foot for at least six to eight weeks, until there is sufficient healing of the fracture. The foot will remain very stiff, and some permanent loss of motion should be expected. Most patients have at least some residual pain, despite complete healing. And, Evan, almost everyone who sustains a break of the calcaneus, or heel, particularly involving the joint, should expect to develop some arthritis. If arthritis pain and dysfunction of the foot become severe, then further surgery may be required. These fractures can be life-changing.'

'Hell, can anything *else* go wrong? I mean, I didn't know that I'd be in pain for ever and then get arthritis. Damn—if I'd known all this I'd nevah have taken Bazza's twenty-buck bet to walk on his ledge with me eyes closed.'

Phoebe used all her composure to refrain from rolling her eyes at the idea of risking life and limb for twenty dollars. 'There are always risks, but I would say that in your case, if you give up smoking immediately, the risks are outweighed by the benefits. What line of work are you in, Evan?'

'I'm a sparkie.'

'So you work with fire crackers?'

'Nah!' He laughed. 'Not a sparkler—a *sparkie*...an electrician.'

'Oh, I see.' She smiled at her confusion. 'Well, you will need extended sick leave to heal, and then you should be back to work without this affecting your capacity to earn a living in your profession.'

'So there's, like, no complications other than pain for the rest of me life and arthritis? Like that's not bad enough.'

'I can't say none, as there are always potential complications associated with anaesthesia, and of course there's infection, damage to nerves and blood vessels, and bleeding or blood clots. But I *can* say that in all of my time as a surgeon there has been none of these when patients follow my pre and post-operative instructions.'

'Like quittin' the smokes?'

'Yes, definitely like giving up cigarettes,' she replied as she completed the notes on her computer so that she could send a report to the referring doctor in an email. 'The most common complications are problems with the skin healing and nerve-stretch. Most wound-healing complications can be treated with wound care. Sometimes—and only sometimes—further surgical treatment may be required if a deep wound infection develops. But most times it is cleared up with antibiotics, and nearly all nerve-stretch complications will resolve over time.'

'So do the plates and screws need to be removed later on?'

'No, they don't need to be removed. They stay there—unless they are causing pain or irritation. Then we can talk about removing them. But we'd make sure there was enough fracture-healing before even considering that, and I've not needed to do it up to now.'

'Let's book it in, Doc.' Evan sat back in his chair and looked down at his injured foot. 'Thanks, Bazza. Your harebrained idea's gonna cost me a hell of a lot more than twenty bucks.'

Phoebe nodded and then completed the paperwork, so that Evan could have the result of his bucks' night antics repaired.

* * *

Tilly had left and Phoebe was just finishing up some replies to emails and wondering where Heath might be when he appeared and answered her question.

'So, how was your day, Dr Johnson?'

Phoebe turned to see him leaning in her doorway. He looked as ridiculously handsome as always, but he seemed to have a sparkle in his eyes that she hadn't seen before. There was still a slight reservation to his manner, but now she understood the reason behind it and it didn't annoy her—in fact it was the opposite.

'Very nice, Dr Rollins. And I have tomorrow off, because apparently your father liked to play golf every second Friday and he has no patients booked in. So I'm looking forward to staying up late and having a sleep-in.'

Heath had been looking forward to seeing Phoebe again. All day he had had her in his thoughts. There were so many things about her that made him want to spend time with her. And she made him see life a little differently. He wasn't sure how long the feeling would last, but at least for a little while he thought he felt whole again.

'Then, since you have no curfew, would you like to join me for dinner? Not at my dad's or at Tilly's. Just you and me.'

'I'd need to pop home and change. Will it be like when we went to Hahndorf last week?'

Heath didn't want it to be anything like Hahndorf. He wanted this night to be so much more.

# CHAPTER NINE

AFTER A QUICK SHOWER, Phoebe put on a pretty mint-green cotton dress and high strappy sandals.

'Finally ready,' she said, passing Heath the car keys he had left on the kitchen bench while he grabbed a cool drink and made himself comfortable on the sofa. 'Sorry I took so long.'

Heath looked at the woman standing before him and knew he would have waited for much longer. He loved being with her. And even being in her home brought a sense of serenity and belonging to him.

'I'm not in a hurry.'

And he meant it. He didn't want their time to end. He knew it had to. He would be heading back to Sydney in a few weeks but tonight he didn't want to think about it. He wanted to forget the past and not contemplate the future. He wanted for the first time in many years to feel alive in the moment. And he felt more than willing to break another rule.

Heath opened his hand to collect the keys and her skin brushed softly against his. He felt the warmth of her touch and his weakening willpower disappeared completely. He wanted more. He didn't want to wait any longer. He wanted Phoebe. Right there and right then. Gently but purposefully he pulled her down towards him.

'Why don't we stay here for a while? The restaurant isn't going anywhere.'

Phoebe swallowed, and her heart and her head began to race when she sat down beside him and the bare skin of her arm touched his. Their faces, their lips, were only inches apart.

Phoebe felt powerless to spell out the consequences and risks to her heart at that moment. Giving in to the feelings she had tried to ignore was imminent and she felt a pulse surge through her body.

She wanted Heath and from the look in his eyes focused so intently on her, she knew he did too.

'We don't have to go anywhere at all if you don't want to,' she said a little breathlessly.

He answered her with a kiss. And without hesitation she responded, and with equal desire her lips met his and her arms instinctively reached for him. It felt so right.

He pulled her closer and his hands caressed the curve of her spine, before climbing slowly to the nape of her neck. His lean fingers confidently and purposefully unzipped her dress, letting it fall from her shoulders to reveal her lacy underwear. He lowered his head and gently trailed kisses across her bare skin. She arched her back in anticipation and he stopped.

'Are you sure about this, Phoebe?'

Searching her eyes for permission to forgo dinner and seduce her for the rest of the night, he found his answer as she smiled back at him between kisses. He wasn't waiting a moment longer, and he led her to the bedroom.

He was not leaving before the sun rose. He didn't care that he was breaking another rule. He wanted to wake with Phoebe in his arms.

* * *

Phoebe woke from a beautiful dream. Then, feeling her naked body being held tightly in Heath's strong arms, she realised it wasn't a dream.

She couldn't remember feeling so happy. She felt as if she had just come to life. Like a flower in full bloom on a perfect spring day. She had shed her fears and found something wonderful. It was as if before Heath had made love to her she had been merely existing—not living. Her body was still tingling as she felt the warmth of his gentle breathing on her neck, and she remembered the feeling of his moist kisses discovering her naked body.

She didn't want to stir and wake the man sleeping soundly beside her—the man who had made her feel more wanted than she'd thought possible. The security of being wrapped in his strong embrace was like floating in heaven. And she wanted to stay in heaven for a little while longer.

She closed her eyes and listened to the steady rhythm of his breathing. She drifted off to sleep again, knowing that she had made love with a wonderful man. A man who just needed help to heal. A man who had broken one of his rules when she'd met his son. And if he was there in her bed when she woke, then he would have broken another rule. Perhaps all that she had overheard in the changing room would now be in the past.

Phoebe heard the shower stop and moments later heard footsteps coming purposefully towards the kitchen, where she was preparing breakfast. She felt happier than she'd thought possible. And her breath was taken away when Heath appeared in the doorway in a low-slung towel.

His smile was borderline wicked.

And they both knew why.

'So tell me, Dr Johnson, how did I get to be so fortunate? What crazy man would make you leave Washington and head to Adelaide?' Heath asked as he moved towards her, kissed her neck gently, then picked a grape from the bunch on the table and slipped it into his mouth.

'Let's forget the man and call it serendipity.'

'For me it is—but for you I sense there was something a little more serious.'

'Let's leave it at serendipity—it has a nice ring to it.'

Heath was looking at Phoebe intently, a little concerned. 'Are you sure you don't want to tell me? He didn't hurt you physically, did he? Because if he did and I ever meet him I'll kill him.'

Phoebe saw how upset Heath had become. They had shared a wonderful, blissful night together, and she wasn't sure that Giles's name and his abominable behaviour should be raised, but she didn't want Heath to think it was more than it was—and after what he had shared she suddenly didn't want to hide anything from Heath. She didn't want to lie to the man who had shared her bed.

With a knotted stomach, she flipped the spinach-and-mushroom-filled omelette and mumbled quickly, 'It was a broken engagement that made me leave Washington.'

Heath's earlier admiring glance at Phoebe, in a short satin wrap with nothing underneath, suddenly became serious again.

'Seriously? You were engaged and you left him to come here?'

'We weren't suited.' Her response was matter-of-fact and somewhat awkward as she struggled with knowing how much to say and how to discreetly gloss over the embarrassing parts.

'How long were you engaged before you realised you weren't right for each other?'

'A few months. But we were two different people with

completely different views on life and on the meaning of commitment,' she said, hoping that that would sum it up and they could move on to something more pleasant—like spending more time together.

'So just how close were you to getting married?'

Phoebe bit her top lip. He wasn't going to just walk away from this conversation. She knew it would sound bad, no matter how it came out. If she didn't tell Heath the entire story he might think her views on marriage were flippant—as she'd dumped her fiancé the night before the wedding—when he had lost his wife so tragically. But retelling the story of the bridesmaids sleeping with the groom would be humiliating.

She weighed up which was the lesser of the two morning-after-the-first-night-together information evils. Only telling him half of the story might scare him, but the full story might make him feel pity for her.

Her stomach was still churning and her heart had picked up a nervous speed. Neither was a great option, so she decided to omit the most debasing details.

'It was close to the day—but honestly it was for the best. Do you prefer your tomato grilled or fresh? I'm more grilled in winter and fresh in summer...'

'How close?'

Phoebe paused. Heath wasn't making it easy. He had been widowed, which was a tragedy, but she had been cheated on—which was pitiful. And the circumstances made it even more embarrassing. She had no option. She had to tell him the whole shameful story.

*The pathetic bride-to-be who couldn't keep her man happy so he found love in the arms of another woman... or in her case women.*

'Your omelette cook broke off her engagement the night before the wedding but I had good reason. Very good reason. But I did do it less than twenty-four hours before we were due to walk down the aisle.'

'I'm certain you had a very good reason. I wouldn't take you for the type to change your mind or your heart on a whim. Whatever happened, it must have seemed that you had no choice.'

Phoebe swallowed, and then fidgeted nervously. 'I *didn't* have a choice. It's an incredibly humiliating story... but, in short, I found out that my fiancé had cheated on me the weekend before the wedding. The best man told me and my fiancé didn't deny it. And to make matters worse—not that I thought it *could* be worse—it wasn't just the once. He cheated twice over the same weekend. But please don't feel sorry for me. It's pathetic and embarrassing and I really didn't want to tell you... But I didn't want to lie to you either...'

Heath crossed to her in silence, turned off the gas under the frying pan and spun Phoebe around towards him. He kissed her passionately and without another word scooped her up in his arms and carried her back into the bedroom. Gently he stood her beside the bed, undid the tie on her robe, slid it from her bare shoulders and let the silky fabric fall to the ground.

'The man was a fool...but *I'm* not.'

Heath stayed until just after eight, when he left Phoebe with a kiss at the door and the promise that with her permission they would do this again—very soon. He had a full day's surgery, but hoped to be home by six, when they would go out for the dinner he had promised her the night before.

Phoebe was so happy she could burst. She wasn't sure what the future held, but she had a very good feeling about it. Heath was so much more than she ever dreamt possible—as a man and as a lover. And she realised that if she had stayed with Giles she would have been cheated out of knowing true happiness.

Her body tingled when she walked past her bedroom and saw the bed with its sheets tangled from their early-morning lovemaking. And then she saw her dress on the living room floor and thought back to how he had carried her into the bedroom the night before.

As she soaked in a bubble bath she closed her eyes and thought back over everything that had happened. She thought there was nowhere in the world she would rather be this Christmas. Then she remembered the beautiful tree that was still waiting to be decorated, so she stepped out of her soapy resting place and wrapped herself in a fluffy white towel to dry off, before slipping on some shorts and a T-shirt and beginning the glorious job of putting up her very first Australian Christmas tree.

But first she needed to drag the boxes back out into the living room and then find just the right place for it...

It was almost an hour later that she'd finally finished. It was a huge tree, and filled a whole corner of the room, and the decorations were stunning. Red and gold baubles, tinsel, twinkling lights and hand-painted figurines. And there was also a miniature tree in the box. Perhaps her father had wanted her to have one beside her bed, but immediately she knew a better place for it. The practice—to brighten the faces of the patients.

She had keys, so she would drop it in later and surprise Heath and Tilly.

She stood back and admired the beautiful tree in her living room for a moment longer, and thought to herself how everything was finally right again in her world.

Actually, more right than it had *ever* been. And she hoped in time that she could make things right in Heath and Oscar's world too.

The telephone rang as she was folding the cardboard boxes and putting them by the recycling bin, and when she picked it up she discovered it was Ken.

'I've looked over the paper we were discussing the other night, Phoebe, and I think I can shed some light on those questions you asked me. If you'd like to come over I can elaborate on those areas of research that you raised.'

'That would be wonderful. I can be there in half an hour.'

'Perfect.'

Phoebe changed into a blue and white striped summer dress and flat sandals. Her hair was back in a headband, away from her face, and she slipped on her sunglasses and climbed into a cab, stopping briefly on the way to drop the baby Christmas tree in to the practice. She put it on the reception counter and then locked the door again. She liked the idea of sprinkling the festive spirit around—particularly with her own newfound happiness.

She spent an hour talking with Ken, while Oscar watched his favourite cartoons. Ken explained the benefits of the new process that had confused Phoebe with its invasive and somewhat controversial approach.

'You're a natural teacher, Ken. You should think about doing more of that while you're out of action—and definitely when you're considering retiring in a few years,' Phoebe told him. 'You have a gift for explaining things in an engaging manner, and the medical profession can't afford to lose your knowledge.'

'That's very kind of you, and food for thought, but to

be honest I'm not having much luck engaging with Oscar this morning.'

'Is everything all right with him? He is a little quiet today. Has he been watching television all morning?'

Ken looked over at his grandson. 'Yes, he hasn't wanted to do anything else. He's been a bit down in the dumps. It may have something to do with Heath's talking about returning to Sydney the other day. Oscar wants to stay here,' he replied as he lifted his leg to the ground. 'If only I could find a way to make that happen...'

Phoebe wanted them to stay too.

She looked over at Oscar and lowered her voice. 'Do you think perhaps it would be okay for me to take him into town for the rest of the day? We could have lunch, go to the museum—just get out of the house for a while.'

Ken considered her proposal for only a moment before he willingly agreed to the outing. 'I think that's a terrific idea—if you're okay giving up your day.'

'I'd love to—but only if you're sure that Heath will think it's okay? You know him so much better than I do. Should I call him and check?'

'He's in surgery all day. Who knows when he'll take a break and look at his phone? By the time you get his approval the day will be over. You have my permission as his grandfather and that's all you need.' He turned to Oscar. 'Hey, little matey—fancy the afternoon in town with Phoebe? She wants to take you to the museum, and I'm pretty certain there will be ice cream afterwards, knowing Phoebe.'

They both couldn't help but notice the little boy's face light up as he jumped to his feet. 'Sure would.'

'Then it's settled,' Phoebe announced, reaching for Oscar's hand. 'We're going dinosaur-hunting at the museum, and then we can head to the Botanic Gardens to have a late lunch—and that definitely includes ice cream. But we'll have to stop at my place on the way. I need to pick up a jacket as it might get a little cool out later, by the looks of those clouds.'

Phoebe called a cab while Oscar brushed his teeth. Then, as she was waiting by the front door, there was a knock. She opened it to find an elegantly dressed woman, her soft grey hair cut in a smart bob, with a lovely smile and what looked like a trifle in her hands.

'Is Ken at home? I just wanted to drop this off for dessert for the boys,' the woman said. Her voice was refined. 'I'm Dorothy. I live a few doors down.'

'I'm Phoebe—please come in.'

Phoebe held open the door while the woman entered with the large glass bowl filled with port-wine-coloured trifle. She could see the rich layers of peaches, custard, raspberries and cream.

'I'm sure that Ken would like to thank you himself.'

The moment Dorothy entered the house Phoebe could see that she knew exactly where to go. She moved down the hallway then turned left into the kitchen without any instructions. The woman wasn't a stranger. She looked as if she belonged there. But this was the first time Phoebe had seen her.

She followed Dorothy and saw her open the refrigerator and place the delicious dessert inside. Phoebe smiled. Perhaps Ken had a lady friend after all. He just wasn't sharing that information with Heath or the rest of the family.

While Phoebe waited for Oscar in the hallway, she overheard Ken mentioning to Dorothy that he'd had an epiphany that morning, after chatting with Phoebe, and how he might soon have more spare time, and then he said something about travelling to the Highlands of Scotland.

Oscar suddenly appeared, and with Ken's blessing they headed for the front door, with Oscar's tiny hand in Phoebe's.

'I love dinosaurs!' he told her loudly. 'The triceratops is the best!'

Ken smiled and waved from his chair. 'Stay safe—and have some ice cream for me!'

Dorothy just smiled. But Phoebe couldn't help but notice that it was a knowing smile, and she felt certain after the conversation she had overheard that Ken's visitor was a little more than just a concerned neighbour...

Phoebe asked the cab driver if he would wait outside her home while she ran inside with Oscar to get a jacket. She opened the front door and Oscar raced straight for the Christmas tree. His mouth was open wide and so were his beautiful brown eyes.

'That's an awesome tree.'

'Thank you. I think it's pretty special.'

'I've never had a Christmas tree. Aunty Tilly has one, but I've never had my own tree.'

Phoebe tried not to let Oscar see her surprise at his announcement. 'Well, I'm sure Daddy's busy—and it's a lot of work to put them up and decorate them.'

'I think it's 'cos they kind of make him sad. He gets really quiet when he sees one. So I don't ask for one 'cos I don't want him to be sad at home. But I helped Aunty Tilly with her tree the other day. Hers is really neat too, but not so big as yours. Yours is like the most *giant* Christmas tree maybe in the whole world!'

Phoebe smiled at his wide-eyed innocence. She remembered being only five and how wonderful it had been at Christmas time. Looking up at the sparkling lights and the baubles and the tinsel and thinking that their family tree was the biggest in the entire world.

'Maybe not the most giant, but I think it's one of the prettiest,' Phoebe said as they both stood admiring it.

'Sure is. Does it have lights too?'

'Yes, I'll put them on—but just for a minute while I get my jacket, because the taxi driver is waiting.'

A few minutes later, with the tree lights turned off, they were on their way to the museum. The short trip was filled with Oscar telling Phoebe he knew everything about dinosaurs, and she was happy to see him so excited.

An hour later, as they walked around the displays of giant skeletons, Phoebe discovered that Oscar *did*, in fact, know everything about dinosaurs—she was quickly learning so much about prehistoric times from her tiny tour guide.

Time passed quickly as they moved on to the Egyptian mummy collection, and Phoebe was quickly aware of how much Oscar knew about that ancient culture too.

'Daddy and I watch a lot of TV about this stuff, and he's bought me lots of books too. He's been reading me some ancient books too, from when he was a kid.'

Phoebe laughed. She wondered if Heath thought of his childhood books as 'ancient'. She felt a little tug at her heart as she remembered how Heath had not wanted her to read to Oscar. She'd put it down to him being very possessive. Perhaps being father *and* mother to Oscar had given him that right.

She just hoped that there was nothing more to it. She knew what a dedicated father Heath was, and how he doted on his son. She had nothing but admiration for how Heath had raised him, with equal amounts of love and guidance. Perhaps he didn't want their connection to change. He had every right to want to hold on to those special moments and treasure them.

'Shall we head to the park for lunch?' she asked, bending down to make eye contact with Oscar.

'Sure,' he said, and reached for Phoebe's hand.

She felt an unexpected surge of love run through her for the little boy. She had never thought much about children. It wasn't that she didn't want to have a family—it just hadn't been a priority. But now, feeling the warmth of the little hand slipping so naturally into hers, she knew it was something she wanted very much.

But it wasn't her biological clock ticking. She didn't just want a child. She wanted *Oscar*. He had crept inside her heart.

Just like his father had. Heath had restored her faith in men. In the Australian heat, the ice around her heart had melted too. She had not expected to find anything more than a career change in her temporary home but she had found so much more and it was all because of Heath. It had not been without a struggle, but it had been worth it and more to finally see him break his rules.

They wandered outside and discovered the weather had turned from a lovely sunny day to quite overcast. It was still warm, almost humid, with ominous summer storm clouds looming.

'I think we'd better stay indoors,' she said, with disappointment colouring her voice. She looked up at the dark sky and then back at Oscar protectively. 'I don't think Daddy would like you to go home wet from the rain.'

'No, I don't think he would like that very much.'

Phoebe wondered what they could do. She didn't want to end their day early, but she didn't think the nearby art gallery would hold much interest for her little companion.

Then it dawned on her.

'What if we go to Santa's Magic Cave?'

'What's that?' Oscar asked with a puzzled expression.

Phoebe was taken aback by the question. She may be on the other side of the world, but she'd assumed *every* child would know about Santa's Magic Cave. 'It's where Santa Claus comes every day in December, to meet boys and girls and find out what they want for Christmas.'

'I've never met Santa.'

Phoebe was surprised further at Oscar's response. 'You *do* know about Santa, though, don't you?'

'Yes,' Oscar said with a huge smile. 'I've seen him in pictures and stuff—but not in his own cave. Where is it? In the hills? Is it hard to find?'

Phoebe saw his curiosity was piqued, and couldn't help but smile at his barrage of questions.

'No, it's not in the hills. It's right here in the city—in the department store.'

'Then it's not a real cave,' Oscar said in a five-year-old's matter-of-fact tone, a little disappointed.

'No, it's not a real cave—but it's Santa's workplace when he's not in the North Pole. And being in the city it means all of the children have a chance to meet him.'

'Not *all* children. *I* haven't met him.'

'Well, today you will.'

Phoebe didn't really understand why Heath hadn't tried to make Christmas a happy time for his son's sake, but she wasn't about to say that to Oscar. Heath had been through great sadness, but she hated to think that he would wallow for ever and never let Oscar experience this special family holiday. But it wasn't her place to question Heath. He was a wonderful man, and she assumed he must find the Christmas traditions time-consuming or awkward, without a wife to help with arranging dinner, presents and decorations.

She smiled to herself. *Could she be the one to bring*

*Christmas into their lives?* And keep it there? Perhaps even take the pressure off Heath being both a father and a mother to his son?

'Today can be your first visit with Santa and you can tell Daddy all about it tonight,' she said as they headed for the pedestrian crossing, hand in hand. 'But first we have to have lunch—'

'And ice cream,' he cut in.

'Yes, Oscar, and ice cream.'

Lunch consisted of mixed sandwiches at a lovely café. Oscar loved the egg and lettuce, but sweetly screwed his nose up at the pastrami and avocado. Then, without any crusts left on the plate, they both had a double-scoop chocolate ice cream cone before they headed off to see Father Christmas.

Standing in line with all the other parents, Phoebe felt a bond growing with each passing moment she spent with Oscar. He was an adorable and caring little boy. Heath had raised him with impeccable manners. Without prompting he said 'thank you' and 'please', and was genuine in his gratitude.

He would one day grow into a wonderful young man—not unlike his father. And Oscar would be a young man Phoebe knew she would be proud to call her son. But she also knew that, no matter what her heart wanted, they were not destined to be together for much longer unless Heath changed his plans and stayed in Adelaide with his family.

Heath and Oscar would head back to Sydney in just over two weeks and her life would feel empty without them. It was a sad fact but the time she had spent with all of the Rollins men had gone a long way towards healing her heart.

And her faith in men.

\* \* \*

'And what would *you* like for Christmas, young man?' Santa asked as Oscar sat on his lap on the large gold padded throne.

Mrs Claus was standing beside him, in a long red velvet dress with white fur trim on the collar and cuffs. She was giving each of the children a Christmas stocking filled with candy as they left.

'I would like to stay here, with Grandpa and Aunty Tilly and Uncle Paul, 'cos we don't have Christmas in Sydney. Daddy has to work, and we don't even have a tree 'cos they make him sad.'

'Daddy's very busy, so Christmas is difficult for him,' Phoebe said in a low voice.

'Well, you're lucky that Mummy brought you to see me today, then.'

'I'm not Oscar's mother—I work with his father...' she began. 'Long story, but today is Oscar's first ever visit to see you, Santa.'

'Isn't that wonderful, Mrs Claus?' Santa said with a hearty laugh. 'So apart from staying in Adelaide, which I'm not sure I can arrange, what else would you like for Christmas this year? You *do* get presents for Christmas, don't you?'

'Yes, Daddy always gets me something. It's usually pyjamas or something. But if I can ask for anything...'

Phoebe could see that he was thinking long and hard about his answer. He was taking the question very seriously. Phoebe, Santa and Mrs Claus were all poised and waiting for the long list of toys they expected he would rattle off. As it was his first visit to Santa, Oscar would no doubt have a backlog to fill.

'I would like a bike helmet with dinosaurs,' he finally

told the jolly man with his gold-rimmed glasses and a mane of long white hair.

'That's a very sensible present, to keep you safe while you're riding your bike. Is there anything else?' Santa asked curiously.

'No. You've got a whole lotta kids in line, and they'll want presents. I don't want to take too many and you run out. Then they'd be sad. The helmet's all I need.'

Phoebe signalled to Santa with a nod that the present would be bought.

'Well, then, Oscar, I think we can manage a bike helmet with dinosaurs for Christmas. And Mrs Claus has a lovely stocking filled with candy for you. I don't think I need to tell you to be a good boy—I think that you're a very good boy.'

Santa lifted Oscar from his lap on to the ground, and his wife held out a Christmas stocking for him to collect on his way past.

Oscar suddenly stopped and turned back to Santa. 'Santa—there's another thing I want.'

'Yes, Oscar.' Santa leant down. 'What is it?'

'I want Phoebe to be my mummy...'

# CHAPTER TEN

HEATH CALLED IN to the surgery on the way home. He needed to check his list for the next day as he had an urgent request for a consultation on a colleague's mother, and had no clue as to his availability. As he unlocked the door, his heart felt lighter than it had in many years. He hadn't wanted to fall for Phoebe but he had and he had broken two of his rules in the process. He intended on breaking the third rule, of not sleeping with a woman twice, as soon as possible. Just knowing she would be near him at work made him smile as he walked through the empty waiting room. He knew he should be feeling on shaky ground as his rules had kept him safe, but with Phoebe he was beginning to feel he didn't need to protect himself.

But there had been a strange phone call from his father. One he would deal with when he got home. Apparently there was trifle in the refrigerator, his father wanted to retire and he wanted Heath to take over the practice. It had certainly been a day of major changes. Some he welcomed, but others Heath still wasn't sure about.

Heath thought his father had perhaps gone a little mad from being at home too long.

The cleaner was at the practice when he arrived, and he had piled all the wastepaper baskets in the centre of the reception area to be emptied. Heath didn't see them in the dim lighting and managed to kick them over. He could see the young man, busy in the surgery, with his headphones on, moving to the music as he polished the tiled floor.

He decided to pick up all the paper himself and then remind the young man on his way out to perhaps leave the bins in a safer place. There was nothing confidential—just general waste. Tilly was always careful that referrals with patient details were filed and that anything else of a confidential nature was put through the shredding machine.

For that reason he was very surprised to see the letterhead of another podiatric practice on a piece of paper thrown in with the general waste. It was unlike Tilly. She was more careful than that. He collected all the other waste and tidied the area before unfolding the letter properly to read its contents.

It wasn't Tilly who had thrown the letter so carelessly into the bin. It was Phoebe. The letter was addressed to her. And the letter wasn't about a patient—it was about her. It was the offer of a dream job. As an associate with the largest sports specialising podiatric practice in Melbourne. It couldn't have been more perfect with her qualifications and background.

And she had thrown it away.

His heart sunk as reality hit him.

*This time* she had thrown it away. But what if she didn't next time she received such an offer? And with her credential those offers would keep coming.

She had no roots in Adelaide, or even in Australia. She could leave at any time. And despite their night together there was no guarantee that she would remain in his life. Or in Oscar's. He spent nights with women and never felt compelled to remain in their lives. Why should she be any different?

She had come into their lives and within a few short

weeks tipped them upside down. He could see Oscar growing closer to her with every day, and now his father had announced over the telephone that after speaking with Phoebe that morning he had decided to retire and consult part-time with the university. He had offered the practice to his son. And then he had told him about that trifle again. What was so damned important about a trifle?

Heath suddenly felt overwhelmed. His carefully organised life was going to pot.

As he tried to reconcile his life and find more reasons to return everything to the way it had once been he thought about Phoebe's ridiculous love of the Christmas season. It was completely at odds with his own feelings. In fact now he thought about it, everything was at odds with the way he saw the world. Phoebe was taking his life and without his approval making sweeping changes. Even Tilly had suggested a Christmas tree in their waiting room after hearing all about the glorious tree back at the Washington hospital.

It had to stop. All of it. Christmas was not something to be—

His thoughts came to a screaming halt when he saw the miniature Christmas tree on the reception counter.

Heath was struggling with the control he felt he was losing. Control of his life…and his heart. Looking at the crumpled letter in his hand, he knew he shouldn't feel safe any more. He never should have felt safe with Phoebe.

Phoebe felt as if she knew what true happiness was for the first time in her life. She was falling in love with the man who'd left her bed that morning, and she was already in love with his tiny son. He was the sweetest boy, and a tiny version of his father. Although not so battle-worn.

'What do you say to us buying a Christmas wreath for the front door of your grandpa's house?'

'Is that one of those green circle things with gold bits that you stick to a door?'

'Exactly. What if we buy one for Grandpa as a present?'

'Daddy doesn't like those things. He doesn't like Christmas much. So maybe no...' he said, in a little boy's voice but with the sensitivity of someone so much older.

She suddenly realised that behind his sunny disposition perhaps Oscar was battle-worn too. He just didn't wear it on his sleeve.

Phoebe thought about Oscar's wish all the way home. A wonderful maternal feeling she had never experienced before was surging through her and making her smile so wide and heartfelt. She wanted so much to be a part of the little boy's life, but she had never considered for a moment that he would picture *her* in such an important role.

*His mother.*

It was more than she could wish for, but she felt concerned for the little boy. He had never been able to enjoy a special time at Christmas, and she wasn't sure why, but she would chat to Heath and she felt certain they could work through it. Heath was a wonderful father—perhaps he just didn't see that what he saw as a silly holiday tradition was so much more.

To Phoebe, Christmas meant family.

And now she was beginning to feel as if Heath and Oscar were family too. It had all happened very quickly, but she couldn't help the way she felt.

She had never imagined when she'd left the sadness and indignity of her life in Washington that she would find anything close to happiness. She had just hoped for a respite. For time to find herself and put the pain and humiliation behind her. Love had only ever been in in her wildest dreams. Phoebe would have settled for a pleasant six months and never felt cheated for her efforts.

The joy that had become her life in such a short time was so unexpected. Heath was the most amazing man, and while she didn't know what lay ahead for them she felt certain it was something wonderful.

And he had the most adorable son.

Oscar was so sweet, and Phoebe had grown so fond of him. She thought that being his mother perhaps wasn't such a crazy idea. If it was what Oscar truly wanted, and Heath felt the same way, then one day in the future perhaps it would happen. Life had turned around, and Phoebe felt blessed as they arrived back at Ken's home.

Phoebe paid the fare just as she watched Heath's car pull into the driveway.

'Keep the change,' she said over the sound of the engine, and she handed the driver more than enough for the short trip home. The driver smiled and took off down the street as Phoebe caught up with Oscar.

She wanted so much to throw her arms around Heath and kiss him, but she thought better of it. She didn't want Oscar to feel that she was rushing to greet his father. She wanted any relationship they had to unfold slowly, and in a way that would make Oscar feel comfortable.

Her heart was light with the knowledge that he wished she could be his mother, but in her mind it was important that the little boy knew he would always come first with his father.

'Daddy, Daddy—guess where Phoebe took me today?' Oscar asked excitedly, and then without waiting for a response he continued. 'To the *museum*.'

'That sounds wonderful, Oscar. You *are* lucky that Phoebe spoilt you like that.'

Phoebe couldn't help but notice that Oscar hadn't yet told his father about Santa's Magic Cave.

'We saw dinosaurs and mummies and we had egg sandwiches.'

Phoebe was taken aback that still there was no mention of Santa.

Heath smiled a half-smile at Phoebe. 'Thank you for taking him out. That was very kind of you.'

Phoebe had thought that after the night they'd shared she would not be on the receiving end of a half-smile any more. Something had changed. She didn't know what, but she could tell that in the hours since he'd left her apartment the closeness he'd felt had cooled.

She hoped they could talk about it later. And she wanted to talk to Heath about Oscar too...

'I've put a roast in the oven,' Ken said as they all piled in to greet him. 'And afterwards there's trifle for dessert.'

'What's with the trifle, Dad?' Heath asked in an irritated tone.

Phoebe couldn't help but notice and assumed perhaps there were problems at the hospital.

'Nothing much,' Ken replied in a subdued voice. 'A neighbour dropped it in. They're a friendly lot around here. Someone's always coming by to say hello and check up on me. And I *love* trifle.'

Phoebe was confused that Ken didn't admit where the lovely treat had come from. For some reason he too was not telling Heath the whole story.

Suddenly she started to see that no one was really telling Heath how they felt, or what he needed to hear, they were all hiding parts of the story and telling him what they apparently thought he wanted to hear. Was Tilly hiding her feelings from Heath too?

'Can Phoebe read to me tonight?' Oscar asked his father as they were clearing the dinner table.

The roast had been lovely and the trifle divine, and Ken had had a big smile on his face as he'd eaten it.

Phoebe was clearly thrilled to be asked to read a story, and her smile didn't mask her happiness. But Heath wasn't thrilled. While Phoebe was a wonderful woman, and an amazing lover, he was more than concerned that she was bringing changes into their lives that he didn't think were for the best.

And he also realised that she might not be staying. Well not forever.

Everything was suddenly moving too fast for Heath to consider properly.

His son had never wanted his nanny to read to him. That was Heath's job every night. It was their special time together. It suddenly hit him that perhaps Oscar was becoming too fond of Phoebe, and he didn't want to see the little boy leaning on her when she could soon be gone.

He felt mixed emotions as he looked down at his son. Phoebe's life was in Washington, or wherever her work demanded. And his was in Australia. Oscar might be hurt if he saw more in Phoebe than she was able to give him. Or more than Heath felt ready to ask of her.

Adelaide was a dream. A wonderful dream. But it was one they could all potentially wake up from very soon. The way he'd woken up from the dream of a happy and long life with Natasha. It could all be over soon.

He needed to protect his son.

And himself.

'Phoebe's tired. She's been on her feet with you all day. Brush your teeth and I'll be there in five minutes.'

Heath continued loading the last of the cutlery and glasses.

'Please, Daddy, I want Phoebe to read to me—'

'Honestly,' Phoebe cut in with a smile in her voice. 'I'm more than happy to read to Oscar.'

'No, Phoebe. I will be reading to Oscar tonight.'

As Heath drove Phoebe home she decided to question him over his behaviour. The top was down on the car as they travelled into the city, but the fresh air was lost on Phoebe. She had something else on her mind.

'Is everything good between us?' she asked.

Heath took his eyes from the road for a moment. He saw the look on Phoebe's face and knew exactly why she was asking the question. 'I've had a long day and we can talk about it another time.'

'I think we need to talk about it sooner rather than later.'

Heath pulled up at the front of Phoebe's house. He wasn't sure how he felt, except that he was losing control by the minute. And although he wasn't blaming Phoebe completely, he knew she could never understand the way his life had to be.

'Come inside. We can talk about it for a few minutes. It won't take long.'

'Maybe we should,' he said as he climbed from the car and walked to the front door, before he added, 'But I'm not staying.'

He had been fooling himself to think they could see each other without complications or expectations. He had been swept up in the moment and had forgotten his rules and obligations. Rules that he had created when he'd lost his wife. Rules that he had been ignoring from the moment he'd met Phoebe. He needed to reinstate them.

Phoebe was surprised at the bluntness of his statement. But she put it down to his being tired and thought he might change his mind when he got inside. She turned on the light and Heath's expression grew even more strained at the sight of the huge Christmas tree.

'Didn't they have a bigger one?' he muttered sarcastically, then refused to look at it again.

'My father sent it to me. He thought it might brighten my day. Oscar loved it today, when we called in. I think he wants to embrace Christmas but he knows it makes you sad. He doesn't know why any more than I do.'

It seemed so unfair to Phoebe that other little boys could share Christmas with their families but Oscar, at five years of age, was protecting his father. And she was worried what that would do to the little boy as he grew older. Would he think that his father missed his mother so much that he couldn't find joy even at Christmas? Would he think *he* was the cause of that? There were many widows and widowers out there who still managed to look for some joy in the world, she thought as she closed the front door.

'Oscar's fine.'

'He's wonderful—but do you ever think that you're stopping him from doing what most other little boys his age take for granted? Having Christmas—with a tree, and turkey, and presents, and laughter and the love of family.'

'That's a bit of a sweeping statement without basis, don't you think? He has presents, and we call home to say hello to my father around that time. Don't tell me he doesn't have Christmas. He does.'

'You call home "around that time"?' Phoebe asked, but they both knew it was a statement more than a question. 'You *acknowledge* Christmas, Heath. You don't celebrate it.'

'I don't want to celebrate Christmas. It's just a commercial holiday wrought by multinational companies to get families to spend up, and I won't be controlled as if I have no independent thoughts.'

Phoebe was not sure what was fuelling Heath's antagonism, but she needed to know. He had been so loving the previous night, and even in the morning, but now he seemed so bitter.

She was falling in love with a man who hated Christmas. And she had to know why.

'Christmas is about families, and love, and being together. You can throw away all the advertising and the hype, but you have to see it for its true meaning and what a wonderful day it is,' she continued.

'It's not and never will be a wonderful day. It's a day I dread every year—a day I can't wait to see the back of. It's a day I need to get through, not celebrate. My wife died on Christmas Day, Phoebe. So don't tell me how I should feel about the day. It isn't and never will be a happy day for me.'

He didn't look at her. He looked at his hands and then at the floor. His jaw was clenched and his eyes stared blankly as he stood and began to pace.

'I'm sorry, Heath. I didn't know.'

Phoebe sat in silence for a moment, gathering her thoughts. She understood that losing his wife on Christmas Day had been incredibly sad, but she knew that he needed to move on and be the father to Oscar his wife would have wanted. If he saw the day with dread then everyone around him would see it the same way. As Oscar grew up he too would learn to dread the day he'd lost his mother and, knowing the facts as she now did, he might to some degree even blame himself. Instead of celebrating the woman who had given her life for him.

'You will never, ever understand. I see the way you make Christmas a big event. But for me, for everyone who knew Natasha, the day is filled with sadness.'

'Perhaps.' She hesitated for a moment. 'Perhaps because you're choosing for it to be a sad occasion. It doesn't have to be that way if you can look at it differently.'

'"Look at it differently"? What? Just pretend my wife didn't die and enjoy a perfect *Little House on the Prairie* Christmas? Life isn't like that. You can't make everything right in the world with tinsel and baubles.'

'No, but you can make Christmas a happy time for your son, and for your family and yourself.'

'It's not that simple.'

'It can be, Heath. But you have to *want* to make it happy—and you should try for Oscar's sake.'

'What do you mean? I'm a good father. I take care of him. I doubt that my attitude to Christmas is affecting him.'

'It *does* affect him. He's hiding things from you.'

'What do you mean?'

'Today we went to see Santa. Clearly I didn't know about Natasha's passing on Christmas Day so I took him to the Magic Cave but he couldn't tell you. Obviously he knew it would make you sad. He doesn't know why, but soon he will ask. I wanted to put a Christmas wreath on the door of your father's home as a gift, but he said no, that it would make you sad. He is taking on a role much too onerous for his age. What if one day, in some small way, he blames himself for your sadness and inability to enjoy life? That's a huge burden for a little boy.'

'It won't come to that. He knows I love him.'

'Of course he knows that—but he also knows that you're sad a lot.'

'And why do you care so much? It's not as if you will even *be* here next Christmas. You'll be gone. Back to Washington or somewhere else. I'm sure that Adelaide won't be able to compete with the offers of work that will arrive...or that you will seek out.'

'What are you talking about? I thought after last night and everything I told you that you'd know I'm staying here. If you want me to, I want to be with you—'

'I saw the letter from that sports practice in Melbourne,' Heath cut in as he leant against the doorframe in the kitchen.

'The one I threw in the bin?'

'The one you never told me about...'

'Because I wasn't interested in it.'

'Maybe the terms didn't suit you and you declined the offer, but you applied. They reached out to you. Forgetting what happened last night, didn't you think that as a common courtesy you should have told me you were looking around at other options?'

'But I applied a while back... Before I left the States. Before we even met. Before last night happened.'

'Before we had sex?'

'Before we made love.'

'However you want to say it...' He sniffed. 'There's some double standards here. You sit here and tell me how to raise my child, but you've never had a child. You tell me that Christmas is about family, but your family are on the other side of the world this Christmas. And you want to get close to my son and read him a bedtime story, and all the while you're looking for work in another city? I need to protect my son...from you.'

Phoebe felt a pain rip into her heart. There was nothing

to protect Oscar from when it came to her. She loved the little boy. 'I'm not about to disappear. I would *never* run away and leave you or Oscar.'

'Stop it. I've heard enough. It seems to me that you want to change everything about the way Oscar and I live our lives. Well, we like it just the way it is—so I think *you* are what needs to change. You need to leave, Phoebe. It's for the best. For all of us, and especially for Oscar. I don't want him to get attached and then find overnight that you've taken off, despite what you say. I saw that letter. It was dated a few days ago and you had every opportunity to raise it with me.'

'I told you—it wasn't something I saw as important.'

'And nor is celebrating Christmas for me, so let's agree to disagree.' Heath had no emotion colouring his voice. It was suddenly cold and distant. Like a judge delivering a verdict. 'I won't have a temporary employee telling me everything that's wrong with my life. Take up that offer in Melbourne—it fits better with your qualifications anyway.'

'You sleep with me last night, then end our relationship *and* fire me the next day?'

'I think it's best if you step down. And one night is not a relationship, Phoebe. There is nothing to end.'

To Phoebe it felt like a death sentence to her heart.

She could see his lips moving but she didn't believe the words coming from them. He was telling her to go. Leave the practice and his life and take a job in another state.

She felt pain rip through her. They had shared the most wonderful night and he was trying to find anything as a reason to end what had barely begun.

'This isn't about anything you said. This is about your cardinal rules since your wife died. I know about all of them, and apparently you've broken two of them with me, but clearly you won't break the third. You never want to sleep with a woman twice.'

Heath swallowed and felt his jaw tick. It couldn't have been further from the truth. But if this would push her away and protect his son and himself, then he was happy for her to believe it.

'Fine—whatever. My one-night rule has been working fine for a long time, so there's no need for me to change it.'

Phoebe felt physically sick. Heath had just proved to her that all men were the same. She felt so many emotions building inside her. Anger, disappointment, betrayal and loss. But she would not take it lying down. She would not be told by a man what she should do with her life.

'Has your father agreed to this? He is, after all, my employer—not you!'

'Actually he's not. I am. You see, your talk with him this morning about how great he was as a mentor made him decide to retire and consult part-time at the university. He's asked me if I want to take over the practice. You have put me in the difficult position of uprooting my life in Sydney to relocate permanently to Adelaide, or watching him sell up. That is a lot of pressure that prior to your little chat wasn't even on his radar.'

'Stop being so angry! I'm sure it must have been on his mind, and it's wonderful news. It means you'll be near to your family and Oscar can see them...'

'Oscar is *not* your concern. You seem to be intent on changing everything about us. You want us to be one big happy family. Your way. That is *not* my way—and, again, if family is so important why is yours on the other side of the world? A little hypocritical, don't you think?'

The fairytale had just ended. He knew that a broken heart and humiliation had sent her away from her hometown and he was making her suffer both again.

He had played her for a fool.

'There's no need to come into work again. I'll cover your patients and pay you out for the rest of your contract.'

Phoebe didn't answer him. She didn't want his money. She had wanted his love and she'd thought she'd almost had it.

Refusing to respond to the words he had delivered in such a callous tone, she opened the front door, signalling him to leave. Her heart was breaking as she watched the man who had just shattered her belief in happily-ever-after walk past her. He suddenly looked different to her. Handsome, still—but so cold. She was looking through a filter of disappointment and pain. The rose-coloured glasses lay shattered in a million invisible pieces. Heath would never look the same as he had that morning, when she'd woken in his arms.

'Please say goodbye to your father and Oscar.'

# CHAPTER ELEVEN

'WHY ARE WE replacing Phoebe?'

'She's gone to Melbourne. She's taken up an offer with another practice. It's larger and it has a sports focus. You knew with her qualifications that it was always a risk she would move on.'

Ken searched Heath's face for a more substantial answer. 'Just like that? No notice? Phoebe's just upped and left us? That doesn't sound like Phoebe.'

'Well, I guess you never really knew her, then, did you,' Heath returned.

His anger wasn't towards his father—it was at himself and at Phoebe. He was battling his own feelings about what he had done. And about what she had told him about himself.

'How can you think you know someone in not much more than a few weeks?'

'I knew I was going to marry your mother after one week,' Ken said in a calming tone as he patted Heath gently on the shoulder. 'Some people you just know. And I thought Phoebe was one of those people....'

'She wasn't, was she?'

'There you go—getting all uppity again. I mean, what on earth makes a woman leave without any warning when only a few days ago she was happily accompanying Oscar to the museum without showing any hint of a woman about to defect. Not to mention I know you two were getting close. Perhaps think through what has happened, Heath. See if there isn't something you want to do or say to make her rethink her decision.'

Heath's jaw tensed as he recalled the visit that had triggered his need to send Phoebe packing. He couldn't allow a woman to get that close again. He might learn to depend on her and so might Oscar. It would turn them into a family. And then if something happened—if she left, how would he be able to pick up the pieces? He had been fooling himself to think she would stay forever. Her family, her life, they were in America. The letter was just a wake-up call and he felt grateful to have found it.

And even if she wanted to remain in Australia permanently, there was Christmas to consider. She loved everything about it with a passion equal to how much he hated it. Christmas was too painful and it always would be. Christmas belonged to Natasha and it had died with her. He couldn't bring it back to life. A piece of him had died that day, and he had tried but he just couldn't feel any joy about it. He couldn't be happy about a day that had ripped his world in two. He couldn't join the rest of the world in their merriment and trivialise Natasha's passing.

Phoebe would never understand. Just as his family never would. There was no one in the world who could understand.

Christmas was just too hard. He owed it to the woman who had given her life for Oscar to have more respect than to move on.

Before he'd met Phoebe his loyalty to Natasha had not been tested. But the moment Phoebe had fainted and he'd looked into her beautiful eyes as they'd opened Heath had been painfully aware that she would test him more than any woman ever had. Or ever would. But he wouldn't let himself fall in love with Phoebe. He had enjoyed her company, and against his better judgement he had slept with her. But falling in love was not on the table for him.

He had to be the father to Oscar that Natasha would have wanted. And he had to keep his heart locked away. And he couldn't do that if she stayed any longer. She was too easy to fall in love with. That was painfully obvious.

There was nothing he could do or say to Phoebe. He had to push her away. It was best for all of them this way.

Heath had patients on the two days since he and Phoebe had parted and each day he woke with less enthusiasm than the last. Tilly said nothing, but he could tell by the look on her face that she was just as disappointed as Ken—and a little more suspicious.

'Your three o'clock cancelled, but your four p.m. wanted an earlier time, so I've moved Mrs Giannakis forward. She'll be here in fifteen minutes. And I've rescheduled Phoebe's patients. You'll be working late tonight to get through them all, but they've been great and very understanding about the changes. You've obviously got a double patient load now, but I've been in contact with Admissions at the Eastern and we've worked out the surgical roster to make sure that no one is inconvenienced too much by Phoebe's sudden departure.'

'Good,' he responded, without making eye contact.

'You might have to put in a Saturday next week to do the interviews for her replacement. Dad did the shortlisting last night—there's three of them. I'll email them today, if you'll agree to do it on the Saturday. I don't think there's any other way. I can mind Oscar, so you and Dad can both be here.'

Heath shrugged. His mind was elsewhere. He hadn't even considered the interviews that needed to be set up. He had informed his father, who had obviously passed on the news to Tilly, but he hadn't put any more thought into it. His father must have moved on things very quickly. Which was best, since Heath's mind was on Phoebe. And on Natasha. And the mess he had made of everything.

Getting too close to Phoebe had been a huge mistake for both of them.

'I must say I didn't see it coming.'

'What?'

'Phoebe doing a runner. She didn't seem the opportunistic type. I know working for a huge podiatric practice with elite sportsmen and women is a great break, but the Phoebe I know would have given more notice and definitely not run off without saying goodbye. She seemed...' Tilly paused for a moment and put down her pen. 'I don't know—a better person, and more grounded than that. She actually seemed to *like* us, odd as we are, and I know Oscar liked her a lot. It's sad, in a way, and I'm surprised.'

'She doesn't owe us anything. She's from the other side of the world and she needs to make the most of these offers. We're just a small show in a small town. Why wouldn't she want to take up an offer like that?'

Heath knew as the words fell from his lips that Phoebe would never have run off for a better opportunity. He had forced her to take it.

'Perhaps there's more to it. Dad thinks there is.'

'You both need to get over it,' he said tersely as he looked over his day sheet, ticking off those patients he had already seen. He had to end the conversation. It made him uncomfortable and brought up feelings he needed to put to bed. 'There's nothing more.'

* * *

'So, Mrs Giannakis, how are you feeling today? I can see here that it's been two weeks since your surgery.'

As he slowly led the woman down to his consulting room and closed the door behind them Heath noted the relative ease with which she was walking for only two weeks post-surgery. Phoebe's surgical intervention had obviously gone well.

'It's still sore, Dr Rollins, but I can tell that it's improving a little every day,' she told him as she took a seat. 'Dr Johnson did a wonderful job.'

'Yes, Dr Johnson is a great surgeon,' Heath replied as he loosened the woman's padded space boot then slipped on some surgical gloves before he began to gently unwrap the bandage to reveal the site of the surgery. He admired the minimal surgical entry point and the exactness of the stitches.

'And she's so lovely. What a sweet disposition and bedside manner she has,' Mrs Giannakis said as she leant over to look down and watch Heath's examination.

'Yes,' he responded as he moved her foot slightly to check the return of flexibility.

'I recommended her to my niece last week. Stephanie's a professional netballer and she's always complaining about pain in her feet. She's seen a few specialists, but doesn't seem to be getting it sorted, so I wanted her to see Dr Johnson—but now Tilly's told me she's gone.'

'I'd be happy to see your niece,' Heath told her matter-of-factly.

'Of course,' Mrs Giannakis replied, still looking down at her foot and the slight mauve bruising. 'I'll still be recommending the practice, Dr Rollins, but I thought that being another young professional woman they would hit it off. And I know you would very quickly have found a large sporting clientele with Dr Johnson here.'

The rest of the day went similarly, with Heath seeing a number of Phoebe's patients and all of them speaking highly of her and their physical response to surgery testimony to her skill.

Heath wished his life was different, so that his reaction to Phoebe could be different. He felt powerless to change the way everything had turned out. He wished the manner in which he had ended things had been better, but that could only have happened if they had never become involved.

But they had.

She was irresistible and he'd overstepped the mark. He was angry with himself for leading her on. For letting her believe that there could be more, if that was what she was wanting. In hindsight, he hadn't set the boundaries early on, the way he did with other women. He had let his desire cloud his reasoning and rushed into something that would never last.

Could never last.

He wanted to turn back the hands of time to their meeting and not look into her beautiful eyes when he held her. He should have treated her as a patient who had fainted, checked her vital signs and not looked further. But he had, and he'd seen the most gorgeous woman. And then he'd got to know her more over iced coffee and realised that there was so much more to this slurping princess. She was warm, and sweet, and intelligent, and skilled. And then, when he'd taken her to bed…he'd lost his mind and his heart.

He would regret everything that had followed for ever.

* * *

Heath headed home, trying not to look in the direction of Phoebe's house. He took a longer, more roundabout route to avoid driving past the place where she had lived for those few weeks. He couldn't risk his reaction. What if her suitcases were being loaded into a cab? Would he screech to a halt and pull them from the trunk? Then pull her to his body, claim her lips with his and never let her go?

He couldn't. They had too many unresolved differences. Differences that they could never move past.

He turned left down another side street to take him around the square where she'd lived. Had she left? Would he be faced with a darkened house? Would he slow his car, look at windows with no soft glow from the lamps, and know that the love and warmth was gone?

With a deep breath he left the city and headed along the main road to his father's house. Back to his son.

Heath needed to travel to Sydney to give notice formally to the hospital there. He owed them that. He knew they would understand his need to take over his father's practice, but he wanted to let the Associate Professor and the hospital board know personally.

His flight left early in the morning and he planned on staying overnight. Tilly was happy to look after Oscar for the night.

He travelled light and the meeting went smoothly. While disappointed to lose his expertise, the Associate Professor and the board wished him well. There was little to do but return to Adelaide.

He didn't feel like socialising into the early hours with his peers over drinks, so he enjoyed dinner with three close friends and then caught an eight-thirty flight back to Adelaide. By nine he was at his father's front door.

As he opened the door he noticed that there were no lights on in the living room or out on the patio. He assumed his father had gone to bed early. As he walked past his room he could see a faint glow from under the door. It flickered like a candle. Why on earth, he wondered, was his father in bed with a candle burning?

He opened the door quietly, in case he had fallen asleep. He intended on putting out the candle for safety's sake.

What he didn't expect to see was a woman with grey hair cuddled up beside his sleeping father. Then he recognised her. It was Dorothy Jamieson from down the street. She had been a friend of the family for many years. Her husband had died almost ten years ago.

'Don't worry, Heath, I'll put the candle out before I fall asleep,' she said quietly.

Heath was having breakfast the next morning when his father walked out very sheepishly. There was no sign of Mrs Jamieson.

'And you were planning on telling me about this little fling *when*, exactly?'

'It's not a little fling, Heath. Dorothy and I have been together for three years now.'

'Three years? Why didn't you tell me?'

'Because I was scared you wouldn't approve. You hadn't moved on from Natasha—in fact I know you still haven't. I didn't want to make you feel that I had forgotten your mother. I haven't, and I never will, but being alone won't bring her back to me. I have fallen in love with Dorothy and she loves me. We still have so much of our lives to enjoy. And we want to do it together.'

'So the trifle was made by Dorothy?'

'Yes. She knows I love her trifle, and she wanted to have an excuse to see me while you were staying here. I didn't expect you back until tomorrow, so I asked her to stay the night.'

'So you told me what I wanted to hear?'

'Perhaps. Don't be cross.'

Heath looked at his father and wondered if what Phoebe had said was the truth. 'Does Oscar want a Christmas tree?' he asked.

'Yes, he'd love one but he knows that Christmas makes you sad. So he won't ask for one.'

Heath collapsed back into his chair. Phoebe was right. Everyone was telling him what they thought would make him happy. He had made them into something they weren't and forced them to keep secrets from him.

He hated himself for what he had done. To his family and to Phoebe. She had been the bravest of all. She had stood up to him and told him what he needed to hear.

And he'd punished her for it.

'Anyone home?' Tilly asked as she stepped inside the front door with Oscar in tow.

Heath walked out to greet them. He was still in shock, and feeling more and more by the minute that he had lost the strongest, most wonderful woman he would ever meet.

'Hi, Daddy.' Oscar clapped his hands excitedly and ran to greet his father.

Heath picked him up and hugged him, then kissed his forehead. 'Did you have a nice night with Aunty Tilly and Uncle Paul?'

'Yes—but when is Phoebe coming over again? I miss her. I want to play Snap with her—and maybe we could go to the museum again or the pool. She's fun. I really like her. Don't you like her too?'

Heath's heart fell instantly as he listened to his son and studied the expression on his face. He lowered the little boy to the floor and took his hands in his. He wished he could give him the answer he wanted. But he couldn't. It was complicated in an adult way that Oscar would never understand.

He had broken the heart of a special woman. Phoebe was gone and she wasn't coming back. She would never be back to play Snap with Oscar again. Nor would they go to the pool or the museum. Heath had sent her away. Selfishly and blindly. For reasons that Oscar wouldn't understand.

'Phoebe's gone away to work.'

'When's she coming back?' Oscar asked, with his big brown eyes searching his father's face for the answer. 'I can do some drawings for her. Can you post them to her? Then she'll miss us and come back.'

Heath sat down and put his son on his lap. He knew the answer would not make him happy, but it was for the best. For everyone.

'Phoebe's not coming back, Oscar.'

'She's *never* coming back?'

'No, she needed to go away quickly.'

Heath saw his little boy's eyes grow wider, a little watery, and his lips tilt downwards.

'Too quickly to say goodbye to me?'

'Yes.'

'But I thought she *liked* me,' Oscar said with a furrow forming between his little brows. 'I thought she liked *you*.'

'She does like you, Oscar. She likes you very much.'

His actions had apparently made everyone sad, but Heath doubted it was a call that he could reverse now. Not even if he told her the truth. That he loved her.

'I guess… But it makes me sad for you, Daddy, 'cos you

smiled so much with Phoebe. She made you happy and now you'll be sad again. I don't like it when you're sad.'

Heath felt his heart breaking. He had been so blind to what he'd had.

'Oscar, if you want we can go and buy a Christmas tree. Maybe it would be nice to put one up with Grandpa and—'

'No, I don't want one any more, Daddy. Santa isn't real and Christmas is stupid,' Oscar cut in, his voice cracking a little as he swallowed his tears.

'Why do you say that?'

''Cos I asked him to make Phoebe my mummy. And she left. A mummy would never leave me.'

Heath knew he had been a fool not to let Phoebe make changes to his life. They were much needed changes that everyone else had been too scared to tell him he needed to make.

He had no idea if she would ever forgive him, but he knew he had to try.

# CHAPTER TWELVE

PHOEBE SAT STARING at her suitcases and at Oscar's cheerily wrapped Christmas present, standing by the door. Her landlord had kindly agreed to arrange a courier to deliver the dinosaur-patterned bike helmet to the little boy on Christmas Eve. She adored Oscar, and did not want him to stop believing in Santa Claus. His father could dress it up any way he wanted, but Phoebe still believed in Christmas.

Her tears had dried slowly as she'd packed her belongings over the three days since Heath had told her to leave. Regret filled her heart that she had so stupidly seen more in Heath and their relationship than there obviously had been from his standpoint. His one-night rule clearly still applied. She had broken the others, but that one still stood.

There was no regret that she had come to Adelaide. She had fallen in love with Heath and his son, and she believed in her heart that Oscar's innocent feelings for her were as real as her feelings for him. And then there was Ken. He was equally as lovable as his grandson, and she would never regret the time she'd spent with them both.

But allowing herself to fall for Heath would be a lifelong regret. And one she felt sure would haunt her waking moments for ever. She had completely fallen for the man who'd crushed her heart so easily.

Her airline ticket was booked. The destination wasn't

Melbourne, to take up the offer from the sports practice, although professionally it would have been advantageous to take on the role. Phoebe knew it wasn't what she wanted. She never had.

Nor was she heading home to Washington.

Instead Phoebe was heading to London.

'I don't know what to do!' Phoebe had cried into the telephone to Susy two days earlier. 'I thought Heath was the *one*. I feel so stupid for falling so hard, so quickly, but I've never felt that way about any man before in my life. How could I get it so wrong?'

'Because, like I said before, men are from another planet. They don't communicate in the same language. It may sound the same, it may even look the same on paper, but the emphasis is very different. It's like a completely different way of thinking.'

'You're right. He's just another playboy and he definitely played *me*. I should never have doubted my belief that all men are the same.'

'Why don't you come to London and spend some time with me? We can cry into a warm beer at the local pub and then, after a while, you can start planning the rest of your life.'

Phoebe had sat in silence for the longest moment. She had stupidly thought the rest of her life would involve Heath.

'Phoebs, don't go silent on me,' Susy had continued. 'It's a brilliant idea. I'm wrapping up a case now, and I'm due to have at least a week off, so the timing is perfect for you to get your sweet self over here. I miss you, and I'd love to spend time with you. I feel terrible that I couldn't get to Washington...'

Susy had paused as she'd realised that the last time

they'd supposed to catch up had been at the wedding that Phoebe cancelled.

'To witness my vows that never happened?' Phoebe finished drily.

'Sorry, Phoebs...I'm so insensitive.'

'Hardly,' Phoebe returned. 'It's just that your best friend's life is a series of unfortunate love stories. Only this one will be the last. I gave my heart completely to Heath—now there's nothing left for me to give another man even if I wanted to. I'm done.'

'London would be good for you, then. There are a million pubs and a nice fluffy bed in my spare room that can serve as shelter till you've healed.'

Phoebe was hurting more than she had thought possible and doubted she would ever heal, but she knew she had to listen to her father's advice and smile through the heartbreak until it didn't hurt any more.

'Okay, Susy—looks like you have a house guest. A miserable one, but you know that upfront. I'll book my ticket today.'

Phoebe was sitting on the sofa waiting for her cab and looking wistfully around the apartment that had held so many wonderful memories.

The night that Heath had stayed over was still only days before, and she could still feel his presence there. It was as if he might walk back into the kitchen with his towel hung low and tell her that the man who had cheated on her was a fool.

Now she knew the only fool was her, for believing him. For waking in his arms, making breakfast together, opening her heart and having him make love to her as if they were the only lovers in the world. For planning in her head the life and the love they would share together, wherever in the world that might be.

She had not dreamed for a moment that it was just a fling for him. A night like all the others he'd shared with different women.

She had never thought for a moment, as he'd held her naked body against his, that he knew it would end as quickly as it had started.

Her stay in Adelaide had been short and heartbreaking.

Her stomach was churning with nerves and hunger. She hadn't been able to eat for the two days since Heath had ended their relationship—forced her to leave and broken any chance of a future for them. There was plenty of food in the refrigerator, but as she stared at it her mind raced back to that morning when he'd walked out in his towel and she'd been cooking omelettes. Breakfast had been delayed as they'd been hungry only for each other.

Now she had no appetite. She had been too upset to think about food. There was no point cooking because she knew she wouldn't be able to eat. She hoped that on the plane she might feel differently. Or at least when she landed and had Susy's shoulder to cry on for a little while.

She felt more alone now, as she sat waiting for her cab, than she had when she'd arrived at the empty house all those weeks ago. Then it had been almost an adventure—an escape and a fresh start. Now she saw nothing that would ever fill the void in her heart...the hole he had made in her soul that she'd mistakenly thought he would fill with love.

Suddenly she heard a car pull up at the front of her home. Looking at the kitchen clock, she noticed that the cab was a little early. It didn't matter. There was nothing else for her to do in the house anyway so she might as well be at the airport.

She stood and crossed to the door. Her steps were shaky and her emotions like a tiny boat riding huge waves. An unexpected tear slid down her cheek and she wiped it away with the back of her hand as she opened the door without even looking up.

'My bags are there by the door,' she told the cab driver as she turned away. 'I'll get my handbag and coat and we can be gone.'

The driver didn't answer her, and suddenly his scent seemed familiar. She spun around. It wasn't a cab driver at all…Heath was standing in the doorway.

She froze for a second. Then the anger and pain that had been her only companions for two long days and nights found a voice.

'What do you want? Haven't you said everything there is to say? You couldn't make the message clearer or hurt me any more if you tried.'

'I'm so sorry, Phoebe. I've been the biggest idiot.'

'Don't do this, Heath,' she said, shaking her head. 'I don't want to play games. You made it clear how you felt. And I'm not about to waste a minute longer with you and your stupid rules.'

'I never paid attention to those rules once I met you. I just agreed with you so that you would walk away.'

Phoebe met his gaze. She wanted to look at the man who had shattered her dreams one more time. She wanted the image to burn into her heart so she could walk away and never be hurt again.

Her eyes were empty. She had cried the last tear on her way to the door.

'But why? What did I really ever do except try to make you and Oscar happy?'

'That's exactly what you did—and you did even more than that. You challenged me and stood up to me and told me what I needed to hear. When even my father was too scared to tell me what I was doing was wrong, you did.'

Heath moved closer, but he did not attempt to touch her. He knew she was hurting and he knew he had caused the pain.

'I refuse to let it be too late. I'm here because I don't want you to leave. Not now—not ever.'

Suddenly there was the harsh blaring of a cab's horn on the street outside. The cab had arrived on time. Phoebe jolted back to reality. She was about to leave for the other side of the world.

'That's my transport to the airport.'

Heath swallowed hard as he looked over to see Phoebe's suitcases by the door. 'I'm so sorry I asked you to leave Adelaide.'

'*Told* me to, actually.'

'I was a fool.'

'I was too—to think that you actually cared about me.'

Her voice was flat. The bottom had fallen out of her world and she had no intention of letting him back in to hurt her again. He could not just arrive on her doorstep and expect to waltz back into her life.

'I can undo it if you'll let me. I'll fly to Melbourne and sort it through with your new employer. I'll find them a podiatric graduate. Please don't leave, Phoebe. Don't go to Melbourne. I want you here with me. I don't deserve you, but I will do whatever it takes to make it up to you.'

Phoebe drew a deep breath, suddenly feeling light-headed as her heart started racing. 'I'm not leaving for Melbourne, Heath… I'm leaving for London.'

She crossed the room in silence and, feeling a little unsteady, she picked up her handbag from the sofa.

Heath paused, momentarily stunned by the news. 'London? Why London? I thought you wanted to take up the position in Melbourne.'

'You assumed incorrectly. I threw that letter away because I didn't want the job. I told you—I applied for it before I left Washington, but the moment I met you and your family I wanted to stay in Adelaide.'

Heath shook his head in disbelief at his own actions. 'I wish I could take back everything I said that night.'

Phoebe stepped towards the door. 'Well, you can't.'

Her heart was still racing, her head was spinning, and she needed to get away from him. Just seeing him again, being so close to him made it hard for her to breathe. It was hard to think clearly. She didn't want to hear the concern in his voice. She didn't want to question her resolve to leave and never look back. To walk away from the man who had owned her heart but thrown it away. She felt overwhelmed. Heath was pleading his case but she felt so confused.

She was confused by him, by his sudden appearance and by the feelings that she felt welling inside.

She needed air. Her chest was at risk of exploding, and she felt dizzy. The heat was stifling, her head was spinning and she realised the lack of food had taken its toll. It was a recipe for disaster.

Without warning the floor lurched towards her.

And she fainted into Heath's arms.

Phoebe's eyes flickered as they opened. She looked up to see Heath looking down at her, and felt the warmth and strength of his arms wrapped tightly around her as he held her against his chest. They were both on the sofa.

'What happened?' she asked as she tried to pull away from the man she still unfortunately loved with all of her heart but who she knew didn't love her. He had told her to leave and she was still clueless as to why he was in her house.

And why she was in his arms.

'You fainted…and I caught you,' he told her as he put a glass of water near her lips.

She pushed it away. 'I don't need anything from you.'

'You need water—or you'll take two steps and faint again.'

Begrudgingly she sipped the water.

'Phoebe, I was a fool to treat you the way I did,' he said as he put the glass on the table beside them and gently brushed the stray wisps of hair from her forehead. 'I pushed you away because I was scared. You were like a change agent in my life, and I needed it and so did Oscar but I couldn't accept it. I didn't want to accept it. But I should have. I should have welcomed it, and thanked you for what you were trying to do. And I want to now.'

Phoebe inched away from Heath. She didn't know whether to believe him. She didn't want or need another ride on the same emotional rollercoaster.

'I just wanted to bring happiness into your lives—and Christmas. But you hate Christmas, and I understand why, but I wanted you to understand that you *have* to let go and let your son enjoy the day. One day you can explain what happened. But not now. He's too young to understand. He just needs to be a child.'

Heath nodded his agreement. 'I thought no one felt pain the same way and that I had to carry the burden alone.'

'I think that you are not giving anyone credit. Your father lost his daughter-in-law that day, and Tilly lost her sister-in-law. They would have felt it too. Not the same level of pain, but they would still have been hurting.'

Phoebe's words hit a chord with Heath. Simple words that made sense. He had been so tied up in his own grief that he had not considered theirs. In five years he had not looked through any filter other than his own despair. And now he knew that Phoebe knew him better than he knew himself.

'I just saw them all rallying around to help out with Oscar and they seemed to be fine. Their emotions were in check and...'

Phoebe shook her head. 'Of *course* they seemed to be in control. There was a baby to consider. If your family had fallen into a heap they couldn't have supported you through losing your wife or helped tend to your son. They were being strong for *you*, when they knew you couldn't be.'

'I never thought about it that way. I thought they were fine. *I* fell in a heap, and I had to get back up for Oscar.' His hands were raking through his hair as he relived the darkest moments of his life. 'That meant pushing away memories, but I didn't want to forget. I felt so torn about that day.'

'It's normal not to be thinking rationally.'

'The last thing I remember when I left the hospital the night Natasha died was the Christmas tree in the foyer. I wanted to pull it down—throw it to the ground and break it. It was so cheery, and my dreams had just died in my arms, and I couldn't understand what there was left to celebrate. It seemed so pointless and I resented everything about it.'

Heath drew a deep breath and stared straight ahead.

'My father drove me to Tilly's house and she had a Christmas tree up as well. It made me feel ill to see it, so I left and went home—and the first thing I saw was the one that Natasha had insisted on putting up a few days before she was admitted to hospital. Oscar was only five months old but she wanted us all to celebrate his first Christmas. She knew it would be her last. I swore that night, when I went home alone, that I never wanted to see another Christmas tree or celebrate the day again. There was nothing in my mind to celebrate about the day. But now I know that Christmas is about so much more than tinsel and trees—it's about family. It's about appreciation of those you have in your life.'

'Yes, and Oscar needs to know in his heart, as he grows up and discovers the day his mother passed, that you don't believe *he* was the cause of his mother's death and that Christmas was a day of joy for Natasha. A day she wanted to celebrate with him.'

Heath nodded.

'As he grows older he may feel that he robbed you of celebrating that day by being born. He may decide to take on your grief and resentment over the day. That's a heavy burden for a little boy to carry and a tragedy if he takes it on into his life as a man.'

Heath looked at Phoebe and understood why he had fallen in love with her. She was undeniably beautiful, but she was so much more. She had an enormous heart and a level of empathy and understanding that he had never witnessed before. And she saw life for what a blessing it was and made him want to be grateful for it.

'I thought if I ran away and pretended the day wasn't happening I could block out the pain.'

'I think you magnified your distress by trying so hard to ignore Christmas. It's everywhere. And every time you saw a sign it must have ripped your heart in two and made you hate it even more.'

'I do hate it,' he admitted. 'I can't understand how everyone can go on smiling and singing carols as if nothing has happened. It's the anniversary of Natasha's death, and every year I feel like I am drowning in memories.'

'Then stop fighting it, Heath. Embrace what the day

meant to Natasha and how she would want you and Oscar to think of her—and the love that she wrapped around you both.'

Heath was silent for a moment as he looked at the woman he now knew for certain had claimed his heart. 'How did you become so wise?'

Phoebe looked away. She didn't think she was wise. But she knew that Heath was not the selfish playboy who had pushed her away. He was a man who hadn't known how to deal with the pain from his past. But she was hopeful now that he had clarity, and that he and Oscar would be okay. They could move forward and maybe even one day have their own Christmas tree.

The cab blasted its horn again and brought her back to reality.

'That's me,' she said, and she softly placed his hand back on his lap and stood up to walk away.

She understood his pain, but it didn't change anything. She had to leave. Heath would always hold a place in her heart but she needed more than she thought he could offer.

'I have a plane to catch. But I do forgive you and I hope we can always be friends.'

'I don't want to be friends, Phoebe,' he said, shaking his head. 'That is not why I came here tonight. I mean, of course I wanted your forgiveness—but I want so much more.'

'Heath. I'm leaving for London. This was a crazy dream, and we've both grown, but I think it's too late for anything more—'

'I won't let it be too late,' he cut in hastily as he gently pulled her back to him. 'You've never been anything other than loving and understanding, and I've been so consumed with fighting my feelings for you, and with the denial and grief and fear built up over the last five years, that I was blind to how much I love you. I was scared of loving you. *Really* loving you and then losing you. But love is a risk worth taking, and I know that now. I will never be whole without you.'

Phoebe stilled. *'How much I love you.'* Tears started falling from her eyes again. But these were tears of joy, and she let his hand gently wipe them away.

'I love you, Phoebe. I think I have from the first time you fainted in my arms. I don't want to spend another minute without you in my life.' Heath pulled her close to his hard body and kissed her mouth as if she was his lifeline. Then, dropping to one knee, he continued. 'If you love me—*and* my dinosaur-crazy son—I want more than anything for you to be my wife. Phoebe Johnson—will you marry me and allow me to spend my life making love to you?'

Heath kissed her passionately, and when he finally opened his eyes they were on her. They didn't look anywhere else. Everything he needed was in his arms.

And Phoebe could see it and she had everything she had ever wanted too. She nodded. 'Yes, I will—because I do love you, and I love your wonderful son.'

# EPILOGUE

'PLEASE BE CAREFUL, darling,' Phoebe said.

'Yes, Daddy, be careful. You're up pretty high.'

Balancing precariously on a ladder, Heath smiled down at his wife and son standing below. In one hand he held a large gold five-pointed star with the letter 'N' decorated in red crystals, while the other hand held on to the top railing.

'As soon as I secure Natasha's star on top of the tree I'll be finished.'

Heath's long arm reached over the top of the ladder and placed the Christmas star atop the ten-foot lush green tree that took pride of place in the living room. It was the same tree that Phoebe's father had sent for her very first Christmas in Adelaide. It was the tree that Oscar thought was the most gigantic tree in the world.

They had added baubles with their names on, handwritten in gold, which they had bought at the Christmas market their first Christmas as a family. And each year they had added more—including one for their beagle, Reginald, who had been rescued from the pound and now sat chewing his favourite toy while eyeing the new kitten, Topsy, who lay on the armchair. She was the most recent addition.

It was their third Christmas together, and Oscar was now eight. Each year Heath took pride in putting their hand-crafted remembrance of Natasha in place.

'Tilly, Paul and the girls are on their way over,' Ken announced as he walked into the room with sparkling fruit punch for everyone.

He placed the tray on the coffee table and took a few steps back to admire the festive decorations before he picked up the individual glasses and gave one to everyone in the room. Then he sat down next to Dorothy and she softly kissed his cheek.

'You know, at this rate, Phoebs, I'll be making an annual Christmas pilgrimage to your home Down Under,' Susy said as she sipped her chilled drink. 'This is my third, and it won't be too difficult to convince me to leave the snow behind to sunbathe and swim to the sounds of Christmas carols again next year—and the one after that. A white Christmas in England is quite spectacular, but I would never refuse the opportunity to exchange my Wellingtons for flip-flops.'

She looked down at her feet and with a huge smile wriggled her bare toes.

'Now all I need is an Aussie lifeguard to make my Christmas complete.'

'We're just glad you could make it again this year,' Phoebe said with an equally happy expression. 'We hope you can always share Christmas with us—and I'll keep a look-out for that lifeguard…then you might move here permanently.'

'You've outdone yourselves—all of you. Your home looks beautiful,' Phoebe's father said as he came down the stairs from the guest bedroom, carrying colourfully wrapped gifts he had pulled from the suitcases and handed them to Phoebe's mother, who was arranging them on the floor with the others already there. 'And I haven't seen a prettier tree ever,' he added with pride.

'It's the best, Grandpa John,' Oscar said as he dropped

down cross-legged on the patterned rug, patted Reginald's head and then looked up with a toothy grin at the huge expanse of green foliage, sparkling lights and glittering decorations.

Heath climbed down from the ladder and folded it up against the wall. His smile grew wider as he reached around and gently pulled his pregnant wife against his chest. With a heart filled with love, he said, 'And it's all because of you.'

'No, not me,' she told him gently, with a smile in her voice. 'It's because you were ready to believe in Christmas again.'

'And love,' he reminded her with a kiss.

\* \* \* \* \*

# MILLS & BOON®
## Hardback – December 2015

## ROMANCE

| | |
|---|---|
| **The Price of His Redemption** | Carol Marinelli |
| **Back in the Brazilian's Bed** | Susan Stephens |
| **The Innocent's Sinful Craving** | Sara Craven |
| **Brunetti's Secret Son** | Maya Blake |
| **Talos Claims His Virgin** | Michelle Smart |
| **Destined for the Desert King** | Kate Walker |
| **Ravensdale's Defiant Captive** | Melanie Milburne |
| **Caught in His Gilded World** | Lucy Ellis |
| **The Best Man & The Wedding Planner** | Teresa Carpenter |
| **Proposal at the Winter Ball** | Jessica Gilmore |
| **Bodyguard...to Bridegroom?** | Nikki Logan |
| **Christmas Kisses with Her Boss** | Nina Milne |
| **Playboy Doc's Mistletoe Kiss** | Tina Beckett |
| **Her Doctor's Christmas Proposal** | Louisa George |
| **From Christmas to Forever?** | Marion Lennox |
| **A Mummy to Make Christmas** | Susanne Hampton |
| **Miracle Under the Mistletoe** | Jennifer Taylor |
| **His Christmas Bride-to-Be** | Abigail Gordon |
| **Lone Star Holiday Proposal** | Yvonne Lindsay |
| **A Baby for the Boss** | Maureen Child |

# MILLS & BOON®
## Large Print – December 2015

## ROMANCE

| | |
|---|---|
| **The Greek Demands His Heir** | Lynne Graham |
| **The Sinner's Marriage Redemption** | Annie West |
| **His Sicilian Cinderella** | Carol Marinelli |
| **Captivated by the Greek** | Julia James |
| **The Perfect Cazorla Wife** | Michelle Smart |
| **Claimed for His Duty** | Tara Pammi |
| **The Marakaios Baby** | Kate Hewitt |
| **Return of the Italian Tycoon** | Jennifer Faye |
| **His Unforgettable Fiancée** | Teresa Carpenter |
| **Hired by the Brooding Billionaire** | Kandy Shepherd |
| **A Will, a Wish...a Proposal** | Jessica Gilmore |

## HISTORICAL

| | |
|---|---|
| **Griffin Stone: Duke of Decadence** | Carole Mortimer |
| **Rake Most Likely to Thrill** | Bronwyn Scott |
| **Under a Desert Moon** | Laura Martin |
| **The Bootlegger's Daughter** | Lauri Robinson |
| **The Captain's Frozen Dream** | Georgie Lee |

## MEDICAL

| | |
|---|---|
| **Midwife...to Mum!** | Sue MacKay |
| **His Best Friend's Baby** | Susan Carlisle |
| **Italian Surgeon to the Stars** | Melanie Milburne |
| **Her Greek Doctor's Proposal** | Robin Gianna |
| **New York Doc to Blushing Bride** | Janice Lynn |
| **Still Married to Her Ex!** | Lucy Clark |

# MILLS & BOON®
## Hardback – January 2016

## ROMANCE

| | |
|---|---|
| **The Queen's New Year Secret** | Maisey Yates |
| **Wearing the De Angelis Ring** | Cathy Williams |
| **The Cost of the Forbidden** | Carol Marinelli |
| **Mistress of His Revenge** | Chantelle Shaw |
| **Theseus Discovers His Heir** | Michelle Smart |
| **The Marriage He Must Keep** | Dani Collins |
| **Awakening the Ravensdale Heiress** | Melanie Milburne |
| **New Year at the Boss's Bidding** | Rachael Thomas |
| **His Princess of Convenience** | Rebecca Winters |
| **Holiday with the Millionaire** | Scarlet Wilson |
| **The Husband She'd Never Met** | Barbara Hannay |
| **Unlocking Her Boss's Heart** | Christy McKellen |
| **A Daddy for Baby Zoe?** | Fiona Lowe |
| **A Love Against All Odds** | Emily Forbes |
| **Her Playboy's Proposal** | Kate Hardy |
| **One Night...with Her Boss** | Annie O'Neil |
| **A Mother for His Adopted Son** | Lynne Marshall |
| **A Kiss to Change Her Life** | Karin Baine |
| **Twin Heirs to His Throne** | Olivia Gates |
| **A Baby for the Boss** | Maureen Child |

# MILLS & BOON®
## Large Print – January 2016

## ROMANCE

| | |
|---|---|
| **The Greek Commands His Mistress** | Lynne Graham |
| **A Pawn in the Playboy's Game** | Cathy Williams |
| **Bound to the Warrior King** | Maisey Yates |
| **Her Nine Month Confession** | Kim Lawrence |
| **Traded to the Desert Sheikh** | Caitlin Crews |
| **A Bride Worth Millions** | Chantelle Shaw |
| **Vows of Revenge** | Dani Collins |
| **Reunited by a Baby Secret** | Michelle Douglas |
| **A Wedding for the Greek Tycoon** | Rebecca Winters |
| **Beauty & Her Billionaire Boss** | Barbara Wallace |
| **Newborn on Her Doorstep** | Ellie Darkins |

## HISTORICAL

| | |
|---|---|
| **Marriage Made in Shame** | Sophia James |
| **Tarnished, Tempted and Tamed** | Mary Brendan |
| **Forbidden to the Duke** | Liz Tyner |
| **The Rebel Daughter** | Lauri Robinson |
| **Her Enemy Highlander** | Nicole Locke |

## MEDICAL

| | |
|---|---|
| **Unlocking Her Surgeon's Heart** | Fiona Lowe |
| **Her Playboy's Secret** | Tina Beckett |
| **The Doctor She Left Behind** | Scarlet Wilson |
| **Taming Her Navy Doc** | Amy Ruttan |
| **A Promise...to a Proposal?** | Kate Hardy |
| **Her Family for Keeps** | Molly Evans |

# MILLS & BOON®

## Why shop at millsandboon.co.uk?

Each year, thousands of romance readers find their perfect read at millsandboon.co.uk. That's because we're passionate about bringing you the very best romantic fiction. Here are some of the advantages of shopping at www.millsandboon.co.uk:

* **Get new books first**—you'll be able to buy your favourite books one month before they hit the shops

* **Get exclusive discounts**—you'll also be able to buy our specially created monthly collections, with up to 50% off the RRP

* **Find your favourite authors**—latest news, interviews  and new releases for all your favourite authors and series on our website, plus ideas for what to try next

* **Join in**—once you've bought your favourite books, don't forget to register with us to rate, review and join in the discussions

Visit **www.millsandboon.co.uk**
for all this and more today!